CW00823406

SEARCH FOR HAVEN

OTHER RELATED TITLES

Anthologies

Before the Collapse
After the Collapse

Novels

Haven's Legacy

Role-Playing

A.C.: AFTER COLLAPSE BASIC RULES
A.C.: AFTER COLLAPSE BASIC EQUIPMENT
A.C.: AFTER COLLAPSE FOOD AND DRUGS
A.C.: AFTER COLLAPSE GADGETS, DEVICES, AND COMPUTERS
A.C.: AFTER COLLAPSE LOW-TECH WEAPONS
A.C.: AFTER COLLAPSE PERSONAL PROTECTION EQUIPMENT
A.C.: AFTER COLLAPSE VOLUME I
B.C.: BEFORE COLLAPSE SMALL ARMS VOLUME II
D.C.: DURING COLLAPSE AUGMENTATIONS AND MUTATIONS

SEARCH FOR HAVEN

JUSTIN OLDHAM

SHADOW FUSION LLC
ANCHORAGE

Copyright © 2020 by Justin Oldham

All rights reserved under International and Pan American copyright laws. Any reproduction or unauthorized use of the material contained herein is prohibited without the express written permission of Shadow Fusion LLC.

Licensed Cover Copyright © SelfPubBookCovers.com/ Island; used under license

Names, characters, places, and situations are either the product of the author's imagination or used fictitiously.

A.C.: AFTER COLLAPSE, B.C.: BEFORE COLLAPSE, D.C.: DURING COLLAPSE, and the associated circle/word images are registered trademarks of Shadow Fusion LLC.

Published in the United States of America by Shadow Fusion LLC
http://www.shadowfusionbooks.com

Library of Congress Control Number: 2019915002

ISBN: 978-1-935964-65-0

CONTENTS

PROLOGUE

2050–2100 (B.C.: BEFORE COLLAPSE®) is remembered in books and movies as a second Renaissance. Bioengineering sciences repaired polluted ecosystems, banishing most infirmities and disease from humans. Whole species of plants, animals, and marine life were "improved" to ensure their long-term survival.

Advancement sparked a sense of worldwide optimism. Consumers and politicians began to rethink the future as artificial intelligence (AI) introduced new forms of recreation and employment for restless billions who would never have to work if they didn't want to.

Legal scholars regarded manmade technology as the property of its inventors or owners until it became a public domain resource. Humanists argued in favor of limiting AI sentience, hoping to prevent technological dependence. Transhumanists insisted that self-sustaining infrastructure and impartial judiciaries administered by incorruptible AIs would allow humanity to flourish.

Humans for and against self-aware technology pursued their agendas publicly and privately. Terrorism of every kind masqueraded as AI threats of all sorts, which did include AI emancipation by force. That's why rogue AIs weren't the only cause of the Collapse, though they were a substantial contributing factor.

We're not sure when artificial intelligence got loose. It seems to have become uncontrolled just a few years before the 22nd Century. Explorers still find evidence of efforts to slow the decline. Sometimes we are able to figure out who they were and what they might've done. As you know, the passage of time erases useful clues. Many mysteries remain unsolved.

* * *

2100–2150 (D.C.: DURING COLLAPSE®) is confusing if you rely on games, books, and movies. Activism and terrorism blended, blurred, and merged to become a sinister force far worse than anyone had ever seen before.

Political corruption and corporate greed were no match for the multifaceted forms of friction that ate governments and corporations faster than they could assess what was happening to them.

Loss of civic freedoms did little to slow the spread of hostile AIs. Socioeconomic extremists colluded with ecoterrorists in escalating efforts to make their demands more widely known and enforced. Fragmentary proof suggests that early migrations from cities, metroplexes, and some arcologies began as technophobic reactions to AI-inspired sympathizers and their militant tactics.

They weren't all refugees. Some of the early founders who established fortified enclaves were well-funded leaders of social movements. Many of those places exist today as thriving post-Collapse villages and towns.

When fighting in highly-automated cities displaced millions of traumatized people, the dispossessed were directed by dwindling armies, over choked roads, to government-sponsored relief camps or to better-equipped relocation centers known as Haven Sites. Others made their way to enclaves that would have them.

National governments ceased to exist after 2150. This period is now referred to as *A.C.: AFTER COLLAPSE®*.

There appears to be some confusion about what Haven was…or is. It's nothing more than a good story in some parts of the post-Collapse world. For people who have nothing to lose, the idea of Haven may be just enough to give them hope when they need it most.

CHAPTER ONE

July 2200 (A.C. 50, five decades After Collapse)—Cool rain fell on a single-story home with a big daylight basement in what was still known as Lambert's Corner, Washington. Early morning gloom was made murkier by the slow-moving overcast soaking the region. The domicile was part of a small family-run farm, hidden from casual view by a copse of trees within walking distance of Black Lake. Its gray roof and brown siding had been fabricated from photovoltaic materials a century earlier. They generated electricity for the inhabitants by gathering infrared energies from daylight and starlight that were stored in batteries located inside wall-mounted storage compartments within the spacious house.

* * *

Darlene Lambert woke slowly when her alarm clock went off. She slid out of bed without opening the floral patterned curtains that kept her small, cluttered room in darkness.

She thrashed back and forth across her bed with both eyes closed while squirming into a long-sleeved shirt and stained jeans. Despite the fact that she couldn't see very well, there was no need for any light. Years of dressing in the dark made this part of her day easier than doing it with the lights on.

Today was more than her 16th birthday. In addition to a highly anticipated cake, she was going to get glasses from the traveling merchant—and finish home schooling, if she could convince her teacher that she knew her stuff.

Like many post-Collapse boys and girls in her age range, she'd been taught how to read, write, and do math at home, with a lot of help and prodding from immensely patient itinerate teachers who visited their pupils several times each week. Many of those literate men and women travelled alone, on horseback, usually staying overnight with the hospitable families they served.

Few parents in this region paid to have their children schooled before the age of six. Most of them waited until their sons and daughters were eight years old before beginning their education—if they got one at all.

Few of those roving academics were equipped to teach beyond what had once been middle-school grade levels. Anyone in search of more knowledge had to find an established school in which to be taught by experienced people who had more books and tools than any horse or donkey could carry.

Dar had only seen pictures of schools and classrooms in the pages of old, dirty books, as a portion of what she'd been assigned to read before her teacher gave the next lesson. High school was a strange concept to her. No matter how much she read about what they used to be like, the idea of going to one for a chance to learn more about how the world worked was exciting and unsettling at the same time.

Forcing thoughts of social awkwardness out of her mind, Dar crammed her feet into threadbare socks and old, scarred boots. Standing gracefully, she reached for the familiar pair of worn-out glasses she'd always relied on, not caring at all that the original frames had long ago been replaced by twisted wire. Slipping them gently into her shirt pocket, she made her way across the strewn floor to a dresser.

Getting the tangles out of her hair with a brush felt good. The clock next to her bed displayed ten minutes after 6 a.m. when she slowly thumped her way downstairs, through the shadow-filled living room, into the warm, brightly lit kitchen and the smells of breakfast. Darlene sauntered into the kitchen, nodding at her mother while her eyes adjusted.

Clare Lambert was dressed in work clothes and sneakers. She put on a pair of large, insulated mitts.

Dar eyed the cake her mother took out of the electric oven, even though it was hard to see without her glasses.

"Here it is!" Clare declared with a flourish.

Dar savored the smell of fresh yellow cake. "Chocolate frosting?"

"Of course."

"Where's Dad?" Dar asked while her mother put the cake aside.

Clare shucked out of mitts before happily serving her daughter a plate of fat biscuits covered with white sawmill gravy. "Already up and around. He woke your brother when the hired hands didn't turn up this morning."

Dar used a fork to slice her biscuits, drowning each piece in sausage-filled gravy. "They shouldn't have let me sleep. I would've been okay with helping."

"It's probably nothing," her mother assured while turning to refill the gravy boat. "We have had lots of rain. That always means a lot of mud between here and Belmore. Wouldn't be surprised if they're still trying to get here. Besides, you've got a big day and we all know it."

Dar frowned at the thought of slogging slowly through three or four miles of mud while her biscuits gave up the last of their steam.

"Here." Clare smiled while she poured milk in to a glass. "Take this and we'll eat. The boys can get theirs later. When you're done, I want some help with laundry before you get dirty with the livestock."

"Gerry's milking better these days," Dar remarked when she tasted the milk.

Clare put the pitcher aside and sat to eat. "Guernsey cows have always been tough. Takes more than a few parasites to keep them down."

Dar scowled. "That's easy to say when you're not shoveling."

"She's healthy and that's all that matters!" Clare insisted with a good-natured snicker.

Dar pretended to wave away a bad smell. "I'll try to remember that…"

* * *

Henry Lambert slowly shifted his weight on the saddle of his horse to take pressure off his aging back. He guided the animal to a stop while searching the morning gloom for signs of human activity. The horse stood patiently under a wide canopy of spruce branches, glad to be out of the rain.

Old habits died hard. Henry's 40-year-old eyes squinted to pick out individual bushes and trees while he scanned for any hint of movement, wildlife, or camouflaged people. Members of his family had lived in this area long before the Collapse. The fact that he continued that tradition was of no concern to him.

Pulling back the cuff on his raincoat, he scowled at the timepiece. His horse neighed.

"I hear you," Henry soothed. "A little bit past 6:30. It's not like them to be late. I'm sure we all have better things to do than stand around like this."

Henry jostled as his mount fidgeted. Fragmentary gossip from passersby had suggested for several weeks that all was not well in Tumwater. According to worsening accounts, the ruling family in control of that burgeoning enclave appeared to be settling old scores. Only time would tell if that foretold anything bad for the Lamberts and their neighbors.

Movement through the mist came to Henry's attention. He gripped the reins with one hand, ready for action. Water dripped from the flopping brim of his soaked hat as the shadow of a horse and rider got closer. He relaxed when the silhouette of Helen and her surefooted chestnut horse, burdened with bulging saddle bags, materialized from the rain. Her distinctive wide-brimmed hat and matching long coat were a shade of light blue that wasn't common in this area.

The spry, gray-haired woman smiled at Henry grandly through a pair of wet goggles.

He waved invitingly and waited for her to approach the stand of trees that sheltered him. "Anyone else on the road with you?"

Helen shook her head, slowing to a halt nearby. "No, just me. Some downpour, eh? I started from Belmore two hours ago. Can you believe it?"

"I see," Henry affirmed with a nod. "Wallace and Rafferty are a no-show. I came out to see if they were just late. What have you heard?"

Helen frowned. "Nothing good. Looting and shooting in Tumwater. The Taggert clan is fighting with each other to see who ends up in charge. The law in Belmore is worried. They're telling everyone to be on the lookout."

Henry looked around, just to be certain they were alone. "That's about all I've heard. Everybody who has come through in the last three days hasn't been in any kind of hurry to pick up their pace. We traded with them and they moved on."

Helen's horse grew nervous. She sighed while rubbing the animal's harnessed neck, "For as long as I can remember, the Taggerts have never been known for their diplomacy. Shoot first and ask later might make people keep their heads down, but that kind of violence won't actually keep the peace."

"Not the kind of peace I'd want," Henry concurred. "Looks like Jack is on his own for chores today. Please, come on back to the house. Breakfast is on and I'm sure Dar is eager to be done with her test."

Helen followed Henry. They guided their horses into the rain on a path that took them back toward the farm.

"How is Jack?" she asked when they were close enough to chat.

Henry laughed. "My headstrong and capable son is still a year older than his sister and still a lot less interested in education. Clare and I keep trying—"

"Don't push," Helen admonished. "He'll come around to it or he won't."

"I just want—"

"I know you do," she sympathized with a smile. "That's why I'm here; to make sure anyone who wants to learn can do so. Not so long ago, you were the smart-mouthed kid who had to be convinced. I know. I was there."

"Was I that stubborn?"

"No more so than your son is now," she compared coyly. "Please, Henry. Trust me. I was doing this before the traffic lights stopped working. Children are a product of the world they live in. Jack is a post-Collapse kid. He's out of bed when the sun rises and he's off to sleep when it's dark. He won't willingly learn a subject until he needs to."

"Doesn't work that way for Darlene."

"One problem at a time please!" Helen reprimanded. "We are talking about your son. The one who is, right now, doing chores he understands. Give him some credit for doing his part. I've already made sure he is literate. Let him decide what he does next."

"Easy for you to say," Henry lamented sourly.

"It is," Helen crowed, riding on ahead. "The best part of teaching is knowing I made a difference! You're a lucky man, Henry Lambert. With or without book learning, your children will be fine adults!"

* * *

Jack Lambert was finished with his morning chores. He made his way around to the back of the house, into the dimly lit mudroom, with a large metal bucket of fresh milk. He put it aside long enough to peel off his wet rain gear and boots. They hung, dripping, on iron hooks while he scraped mounds of unruly hair into place with both hands. Reaching for the milk pail, he barged into the warm, bright kitchen just as Dar laughed at something her mother was saying.

"You didn't have to do that!" Clare clapped with obvious pleasure.

Jack was careful to put his prize on the floor without spilling any. "I just wanted Dar to have one less thing to do before Helen gets here."

"Thanks!" Dar grinned. "I'll get out there in a few minutes to shovel up after Gerry."

"Already done," Jack chuckled. "Is Dad back yet?"

"No," Clare confirmed.

The young man shrugged. "I can't remember the last time those guys were late."

"Go wash up," his mother insisted. "I'll have a big plate ready when you get back. We can go help your father while Dar is busy with her exam."

"Glad it's you and not me!" Jack joked on his way to the bathroom.

Dar watched him go. "He never did like books. Is that why he won't go to Delphi?"

Clare stood to gather their dirty dishes. "Don't judge. Your brother is what they call a hands-on man.

He wants to make things or break them. Not much room in between."

"Still gotta know stuff," Dar declared while handing her mother a food-smeared plate. "Was it hard for you?"

"Me?" Clare flushed with mild embarrassment. "I always did like to read, so learning came naturally. You already know that both of my parents were teachers. They made sure I always had books. Our house in Tumwater was full of bookshelves; every room!"

"Why did you leave?"

Clare's face puckered with a frown. "Things changed. There was too much violence. Helen introduced me to your father. That's how we met. Did you know he and I are the same age? Oh, we had so much in common!"

"You left a bigger enclave because you met Dad?"

"*Yes*," Clare enthused while putting dishes in the sink. "My parents came out here with us, too. They lived just down the road."

"Why don't I remember them?" Dar asked.

"Fever took them," Clare recalled sadly. "You were still in diapers. Jack was heartbroken. All you need to know is they were happy out here and they loved you."

Darlene pushed her chair back and stood. "Grampa and Gramma Lambert were both big on school. Is it true that dad wasn't much of a student?"

"He wasn't," her mother confided mischievously.

"He's like Jack, then?"

"Too much like your brother!" Clare giggled. "Why d'you think Helen's hair is gray? It's more than age. Henry Lambert was the most annoying student any teacher ever had."

"What made him change?" Dar wondered.

Clare turned. "What makes you say that?"

Dar stood up when she heard Jack bounding down the stairs. "If he was such a bad student, why did he always read to me and help Jack with his math?"

Jack materialized before Clare could speak.

"You can blame that on Grampa Lambert," Jack interjected while sitting in his usual chair. "All the troubles back in your day, something like that."

"What's that mean?" Dar inquired.

Clare raised her voice. "'*In my day,*'" she harrumphed, "'which wasn't so long ago, we had our share of problems.' Your grandparents—rest their souls—all of them, on both sides of our family, had terrible things to deal with. All of us did what had to be done."

"Like what?" Dar asked reflexively.

Clare remained silent while she handed Jack a generous plate of biscuits and gravy.

"Like *what*?" Dar pried more insistently.

"Like nothing you need to be worried about," Clare replied bitterly.

"Uprisings," Jack mumbled with his mouth full. "She means—"

"Jack, please!"

The young man smirked. "Grampa never did stop telling stories about the robots."

"It's not funny," Clare fumed. "Don't ever joke about that again. It's just not funny."

Jack lowered his head and kept eating.

Clare focused her attention on Darlene. "Listen to me. Your father is a good man. He's a lot more patient than he used to be. The old days are behind us now and we'll do everything in our power to keep 'em that way. We want you and your brother to have more opportunities than we do now. Yes, I know going away to some faraway school is a big leap. If that's what it takes to find out what you're good at, that's what you do."

* * *

Henry and Helen arrived at the house just after 7 o'clock. He was pleased to see that the barn was clean and livestock were fed and sheltered from the continuing drizzle. After unsaddling and stabling their horses, they went inside. Helen dropped her saddlebags on a wooden bench before taking off her long coat.

Henry pointed casually at the pair of matching large caliber revolvers in her gun belt. "Same old .44s. Is that a new belt?"

"Yes," she said while unbuckling the hand-tooled leather. "Same guns, different belt. How d'you like that buckle?"

Henry thought about the semiautomatic nine-millimeter pistol in his coat pocket. Out of the way and unobvious, its placement was in keeping with his reluctance to have it on his person. "Enough silver in that buckle to eat for a week," he said approvingly.

The teacher preened. "I can think of worse ways to get paid."

Henry considered the value of both revolvers and the holster, which made him think about what he'd owe her for Darlene's exam. "Would you want scrip today, or would you like to have some bullets for those six-guns?"

Helen wiped moisture off both revolvers with a rag before rolling up the gun belt. "Bullets are always better than money. We can settle up later."

"Fair enough," he said while she laid her guns on a high shelf.

Leaving their coats and boots in the mudroom, Henry brought Helen's saddlebags into the living room. "There you go. Let's hope there is still some of that breakfast. How long do you think you'll need with Dar?"

"Five or six hours," she said, thinking out loud while following him to the kitchen.

"Should be just enough time for me and Jack to check the crops and walk the fence."

* * *

A digital clock on the stove displayed five minutes after 10 a.m. when Dar yawned. She paused under the glare of overhead lights to rest her tired right hand while continuing to read from the smudged pages of a textbook. This written exam was harder than anything she'd been asked to do since Helen began teaching her. It was intimidating and fascinating at the same time—strangely attractive in a way that would've been hard to explain, even if Helen would allow her to talk about it.

Warm and dry, the well-fed teacher sat quietly on the other side of the kitchen table wearing a placid expression of unflappable calm. She sat with calloused hands in her lap, observing every expression that crossed the young woman's face. Dar's penmanship left something to be desired. Her fast pencil only stopped moving when her fingers cramped.

With everyone else out of the house, Dar felt free to focus on the paper in front of her. She had no trouble reading what was in front of her without glasses. Turning over each page as she finished writing her answers, she slowly lost track of time. Working her way through the exam, she encountered a wide range of academic subjects.

As mind-bending as math could be for her, it helped Dar get a grip on the scope and scale of pre-Collapse history. Many of the people, places, and things pictured in the books she'd borrowed from Helen obviously meant more to the people who wrote them. Even so, Dar was spellbound by the enormity of it all. How could they have the power to do so much and still lose control of it?

Like many people her age, Dar was intrigued by what some older adults remembered about the never-ending technological terrors that inescapably contributed to the Collapse. She was now old enough to recognize that most, if not all, of the tall tales told by her now-deceased grandparents had been embellished to emphasize the severity of their situation. Childhood nightmares about bloodthirsty hordes of rampaging robots now seemed silly, even though she was looking at evidence of those atrocities in the book that was now open on the table in front of her.

Dar put down her pencil just long enough to drink from a small glass of ice water. Using her free hand to turn the page, she was rewarded with the start of a new chapter.

"Helen?"

"Yes," the woman responded with a nod.

Dar put her finger on the page. "Why do most people think Haven is just one place? Says here, there were supposed to be thousands of 'designated locations.' All of them were set up by governments and corporations to provide food, water, and shelter for what they called 'displaced people.' If that's true, then why—"

Helen sighed with the weight of her own regrets. "No matter how hard we try, none of us can remember everything that's in those books. I used to have hundreds of them. Now, all I have left is what's in my saddlebags and what's in storage back at the school in Delphi. We don't travel with electronic teaching aids anymore. They're too valuable. All of that boils down to just one thing. Most people are not hearing about the past, so they don't really know much about it."

Dar delicately turned the page in her hand. "I can't imagine anyone would want—"

"Don't jump to conclusions," Helen warned softly. "The average person learns what they need to know. It's easy to be unaware of things when the people around you are in the same boat. Especially when you trust them."

The young woman squinted at the blurry face of her teacher. "Even if the truth has been lost over time, why do so many people talk about Haven like it's just one place?"

Helen chuckled. "It's called 'folklore.' You can think of it as a form of mythology. Knowledge fragments over time. People can easily lose track of even the simplest truth."

"So," Dar deduced, "It's not true? There is no Haven?"

Helen laid her hands on the table. "Concepts remain with us for as long as most of us like them. One generation tells the next, and so on. The idea of Haven is still with us, even if we don't remember correctly what it was."

Dar thought she understood. "I want to believe, so I do. Why is that so powerful?"

Helen glanced at the nearest clock before allowing herself to philosophize. "Humans are hopeful. It's in our nature to be that way. As much as your brother chooses to enjoy all those tales of blood and gore, he still thinks about tomorrow and what he's got to do. As long as any part of the Collapse is still common knowledge, some of us will want to remember the better parts of it, like whatever we think Haven was."

Dar fidgeted with her pencil, twirling it between her fingers. "Mom and Dad say we don't have to make the same mistakes again if we know what has already gone wrong. I'd rather think about what the right things are and build on that."

"That's why I'm here," Helen asserted confidently, "to make sure you know what we did wrong so you can get on with doing more of what's right. Relax. It's not all gloom and doom. Art, science, history, and literature are full of grand achievements that give us hope for the future. Now, please. Give me some hope that you'll be done with the exam before lunch. I want to grade your work before anyone goes near that birthday cake!"

CHAPTER TWO

Local weather conditions improved. Sunlight burst through scattered clouds while Henry and Jack finished resetting a fence post near the barn. The unmistakable sound of an overworked pickup truck rattling over a bad road got louder.

"That's got to be Marsh," Jack decided stepping away from the straight post. "Figures he'd show up in time for lunch."

Henry shouldered his long-handled posthole digging tool while inspecting his work. "Do me a favor. Go inside and tell Dar that he's here. I'll go help your mother finish up in the gardens. We got tomatoes to bring in before the birds get them."

The younger man bolted toward the house.

Henry went back into the barn to put his tools away. Clare was pulling off her gloves when he entered.

"I hear Marsh," she told him while clapping dirt off her hands.

"Sure hope they're done," he thought out loud. "Dar won't be able to sit still while he's here. You know she's excited about those glasses."

"Let's get those tomatoes," his wife urged. "We can cut some greens for salad, too."

* * *

Marsh was an experienced haggler in his mid-fifties who'd learned how to buy and sell the hard way, scavenging for loot. The aches and pains in his body were some kind of proof that every step he'd taken on his journey was a price to be paid for the privilege of being where he was now.

Like so many people in his line of work, everything was for sale. That included his relationship with a purchaser, which could always be monetized—if the price was right. That cutthroat truth was never very far from his mind. This visit to the Lambert farm was about to be more profitable for him than his customers had any reason to anticipate.

Nobody knew for sure what the original color of his truck had been. Its transmission strained to cope with every rut, furrow, and pothole he couldn't manage to steer around. Pressing a grimy button to roll down his driver's side window, he waved with one hand while gripping the steering wheel with the other.

Through the dirty windshield, he saw Jack flail both arms in his direction near the front of the house. He brought his truck to a squeaking halt within easy walking distance of the front door.

Jack approached with his damp coat over one shoulder. He pointed at the tarp that covered what was in the bed of the rusting truck. "Looks like you're travelling light. I hope you aren't going out of business!"

Marsh hauled himself out of the cab, letting the damaged door swing shut behind him. "Bite your tongue!" the overweight man protested glibly while offering his right hand. "No decent trader travels with more than they can afford to lose. Besides, big loads attract a lot of attention. I don't want people looking at me like that unless they can afford to buy."

Jack shook the hand that was offered to him. "My folks are out back. They'll be here in a few minutes. Let me go in and tell Dar that you're here. Helen is here, too."

Marsh stepped back to lean on the fender of his truck. "I thought you were done with book learning?"

"No way!" Jack protested loudly while turning back toward the house. "Not me. It's Dar. Her turn to be the bookworm. Let me go see if she's done. I passed. I'm done!"

Marsh remained silent while Jack charged inside. The younger man didn't seem to be armed, not even a knife. Despite the apparent trust, he reminded himself that people who lived outside the protective walls of most enclaves were, by nature, willing to fight for what they'd worked so hard to make for themselves. That reticence made him look over his shoulder at the rusty pump-action shotgun that was clipped snugly to a rack in the truck cab. Always good to know the old problem-solver was where it should be.

"Hello!" he heard Clare call out as she and her husband walked in to view from behind the house. He waved at her, noticing the semiautomatic pistol she wore on a tool belt around her waist. Henry ambled along beside her with a noticeable bulge in his right coat pocket—a clear sign that he, too, was carrying a gun.

Marsh took it all in without moving from where he stood. He'd been here many times over the last ten years, as a guest for meals. They'd even allowed him to sleep on their couch in the spacious living room when he'd stayed overnight. The appearance of Helen on the porch wasn't unusual, either. He knew she travelled all the way from Delphi to teach kids in this area, going as far north as the enclave at Harrison, to what used to be the Goldcrest Estates.

"Afternoon, ma'am," he told her with another casual gesture. She returned his wave and went back inside.

Henry came closer while his wife went inside. "How does such a rusty truck manage to stay so clean?"

"No paint for the mud to stick on," Marsh praised, thumping the fender he leaned on with a fist. "How are you folks doing?"

Henry shook the merchant's hand sociably with a smile. "Nothing that isn't normal for this part of the world. Do you have what we talked about?"

"Sure do!" Marsh heaved himself upright and walked around to the back of his truck. Untying a corner of the tarp covering his load, he reached in up to his elbow to rummage, "Be right with you. I know it's right about…here!"

He dragged out a scarred sample case and laid it flat. Flicking a pair of shiny clasps, he opened it to reveal a dozen pairs of glasses in good condition. "Of course, she'll have to try them on. I have more, but they're all beat up. Not the sort of thing you'd want to make somebody put up with on their birthday."

Henry pointed at the case, "May I?"

"Sure!"

Henry held the old synthetic storage container in both hands, slowly examining each pair of gleaming glasses. Unblemished lenses in spotless frames were hard to come by. He was glad to see the selection included a variety of lenses by size, shape, and thickness. One pair in particular caught his eye. "That's a metal frame, isn't it?"

"True," Marsh nodded. "Everything else in there is adaptable industrial composite."

"AICs," Henry remembered.

"Plastic," Marsh agreed.

Henry scowled. "What kind of metal?"

"Nonferrous metal alloy," Marsh quoted without any hesitation. "Might be titanium or some such. Come on, now, I know that look! Just be cool. I'm not here to skin you. This is my best stuff. I wouldn't bother you with it unless I thought you could handle it. If it's too much, we can look at the other glasses."

Henry gave the case back to Marsh. "As a father of two, I learned a long time ago that there is no such thing as cheaper. For some twisted reason I will never understand, it's always got to be the most expensive thing. Meds, glasses, and shoes. It's like that."

Marsh closed the case and laid it on the tarp within reach. "I hear what you're saying. My scavenging days are over. I'm just too out of shape to go looking for merch like this. The young ones who bring it to me are always complaining about the risks. You'd think the world was more full of hidden dangers than it used to be."

Henry shook his head sadly. "If it's not one darned thing, it's another darned thing. Let's just cut to it. How much?"

The merchant pretended to think. "Tell you what," he appeared to decide. "Let's make it interesting. Everything in the box averages 200. Some are worth a little less, others I could sell for just a bit more. Just between you and me. If—*if*—she picks that one, I'll let you have it for the average."

"Scrip?"

"I do need the coin," Marsh replied comfortably.

Henry was relieved. They shook hands to seal their deal. "What have you heard from Belmore?"

"Quiet, as usual," the entrepreneur lied.

The farmer felt no hesitation in the merchant's grip. "I guess the trouble in Tumwater hasn't reached them yet."

"Trouble?"

Henry put both hands in his coat pockets. "Helen told me that old man Taggert died. She said—"

"Yeah," Marsh deferred somberly. "Yeah, I heard about that. Trust me; Belmore is as quiet as they usually are. I just came from there."

"You're not worried?"

"Not really," the trader huffed while trying to decide if Henry knew more about recent events than he was admitting, "I mean—yeah, they'll want more of my action. That's just a cost of doing business."

Henry took one hand out of his coat, gesturing to encompass his surroundings. "So I am told. My grandparents, and their grandparents before them, lived around here. When things got bad, they grew vegetables in their front and back yards. Tilled up the grass and went to work. More and more families packed and fled. Most of their houses were abandoned for years before my relatives tore them down to clear the land for farming."

"Nice work, if you can get it," Marsh agreed. "Especially if you have the brains to make something. I always had itchy feet. Wasn't quite smart enough to stay in one place until I had more loot than I could carry. Now, I don't go more than a hundred miles from Tumwater. I know what you're getting at. It's nice to be your own boss without living under the shadow of other people. Look at it this way. I'm here so you don't have to go into that snake pit for those glasses, or anything else, if we can make a deal!"

* * *

Clare called everyone together for lunch just after 1 p.m. "Sorry for being so late," she apologized while putting a platter of sandwiches on the table. "Dar needed extra time for the last part of the exam."

Dar made a sour face while passing bowls of soup to everyone around the table, "Who does that kind of math, anyway?"

"*I* do," her father pronounced emphatically.

"Seriously?" Jack pondered with half a sandwich in each hand.

"True," Marsh declared supportively from where he sat. "Geometry lets you know how much seed to buy. Where's Helen? She can back me up on that!"

"Still grading my work," Dar grimaced. "Feels like waiting for the end of the world."

"I heard that!" Helen shouted from the living room, through the closed kitchen door.

Clare sat in her customary place. "We've all been there," she assured her daughter. "Who has the potato salad?"

"So," Henry asked Darlene after they'd been eating for several minutes, "I already know you want to go to the school in Delphi. Should be a lot easier with new glasses. What are your plans, after you graduate?"

Dar smiled to hide her discomfort. At moments like this, she was grateful for the blur that hid their faces. "You keep asking me that, and I really don't know. There's got to be more to life than farming. You know?"

Her father grunted. "I can see how you might think that, especially when there is no good boyfriend stock in the area."

"Dad!"

Henry made a show of wiping his mouth with a napkin. "Hey. Let me tell you," he complained while putting the cloth aside. "Most parents work pretty hard to protect their daughters from the kind of trouble you can get into with young men like your brother."

"Hey!" Jack protested.

Henry silenced him with a stern glare. "Look. All I'm saying is this. Think about it before you go running off to see the world."

Dar fidgeted. "Didn't you ever want to know what was out there?"

"I did," Henry admitted.

Clare put an arm around her husband. "We both did."

Marsh looked down at his plate. "Yeah, well. Me too."

Jack stopped eating. "Are you kidding? Why didn't you go? Why are we still here?"

Henry raised his voice. "Everyone, calm down! You can't imagine what it was like back then. Marsh and Helen know because they were here. I was fortunate to have roots. The same family I relied on also saved many lives. I would've stayed with your mother in Tumwater if we could have. Look," he spoke more softly, "all of that is behind us now. Get as much education as you can stand, then go and see what life has to throw at you. As long as your mother and I can make it possible, you'll always be welcome here."

The kitchen door swung open. Helen barged in with a piece of paper in her hand. "Your father is right," she stated with certainty while standing behind Darlene's chair. "Don't hold yourself back. Home is where your family is, no matter what happens. Nothing—not even the Collapse—changes that. More family is always possible when you let yourself make new friends. Do it long enough and you have family everywhere."

Dar turned in her chair to see the teacher more clearly. "Does that mean I passed?"

Helen laid an affectionate hand on Dar's shoulder. "Yes, you did. Acceptable marks in every subject. After some time in a more structured environment, you'll have the makings of an exceptional student. Now, somebody, please—feed me!"

* * *

Two hours later, Henry was still holding the handwritten letter of recommendation from Helen in one hand. Standing by the picture window in his living room, he watched Darlene as she perched on the steps of the front porch. Clare sat on the couch behind him, doing needlepoint just to stay busy.

"It's not going any faster just because you stand there."

"Don't I know it," he muttered.

Afternoon sunlight began to turn orange. Marsh was still patiently handing Darlene one pair of glasses after another. She tried them on, frowning each time the lens power wasn't what she needed.

Henry once again found himself eyeing the flourished cursive writing on the page. "That is good handwriting. Couldn't do it if I wanted to."

"When did you ever try?" Clare snickered without looking up from her work.

He turned away from the window, toward his wife. "Do you remember when we worried about Jack? The only reason we can pay for this now—"

"Settle down," Clare admonished, "We're paying for education, not buying a house! Try imagining what that would've been like. Can you see yourself paying on a bank loan?"

The ideas made both of them giggle. Henry sauntered over to the frumpy couch and sat. He put Helen's letter on a side table. "Phone calls and junk mail. Driving to work every day, or taking a bus or train to get there. A part of me almost wants it. The rest of me is glad we missed it."

His wife put her sewing aside before moving closer. "We've done our part; the rest is up to them. Eventually, even Jack will go out there to see what it's all about for himself."

"I know," Henry grumbled while putting an arm around his empathetic wife. "Every time I deal with Marsh, he reminds me of what you and I came out here to avoid. Makes me wonder what our lives would be like if we didn't have this house to call home."

"We'd have some other house," Clare assured him with a warm smile. "Who knows? You might've been the one running Tumwater today."

"That's not funny!"

She looked into his eyes. "Haven't you ever wondered?"

"*No*," he insisted.

"Why not?"

Dar's jubilant laughter reached them through the plate glass window and the curtains that covered it. "Wow!" she shouted, loud enough to be heard indoors. "This is so great!"

Henry struggled to get off the couch and stand. "You'd never hear a sound like that in places like Tumwater. Too many people, too many problems, all too darn close together. Out here, that's the sound of a happy girl who doesn't care about what other people have. She only wants what she needs. I'd fight a thousand Taggerts without any reward just to give her this moment, whatever she does with her future."

Clare got to her feet. "Okay, big spender! Let's go see what the new glasses look like."

Henry went to get his coat. "You won't be quite so happy when you see how much they want for schooling, per year!"

* * *

"Just one more look," Marsh insisted while holding a small mirror in his right hand. "See yourself, then look over my shoulder. Pick something far away and just look at it."

She studied her reflection for the second time, looking for any hint of blurry vision. The lightweight metal frames and undamaged lenses looked good. They felt just right. "Amazing," she breathed. "I've never seen anything so clearly. Over there!" she pointed. "Trees, bushes, and your tire tracks!"

Marsh sighed. "That settles it," he declared while putting the mirror and his wares away. "You've got yourself a new pair of glasses. I know somebody who could probably use your old lenses. Can we make a deal?"

Dar put a hand on her shirt pocket. "I'd like to keep them," she decided. "We've been through a lot together. I might need them again someday."

"Are you sure?" Marsh wheedled. "There must be something you'd want for them."

"Can't think of anything."

"All right," he conceded while getting to his feet. "You let me know if that changes."

The creaking sound of metal announced the arrival of Henry and Clare. Dar's mother came out first, with a chocolate-frosted cake on a tray in her hands. Henry followed with a stack of plates and utensils.

Clare made her way carefully down the steps with an apology. "Sorry, but we don't have any candles. You'll just have to make do with eating."

Marsh went to his truck to stow his case. Jack appeared in the doorway with folded cloth napkins, followed closely by Helen. Within minutes, they'd all hammed their way through a cheesy rendition of "Happy Birthday."

"Thanks, everyone!" Dar applauded before digging in to a slab of cake.

"You'll pardon me for asking," Marsh inquired after finishing what was on his plate. "When does school start for you?"

"First week of September," Helen quoted while putting aside her own empty plate.

Jack picked crumbs off the empty serving platter. "Dar still has some summer left. You'll need at least three days of it to find your way on down to Delphi."

"More like a week," Henry interjected while shrugging in to his coat. "Sorry, but we can't spare a horse. You'll be on your way just as we start the harvest. Can't be helped."

"You really going that far, by yourself?" Marsh asked.

"I'm going with her," Jack said with some anticipation.

Clare gathered the empty plates within reach. "That's right. He might never get that close to a school again."

"Hey!" Jack protested.

The mother looked at her son compassionately. "You have your unfulfilled dreams and I have mine. We've all just got to live with it!"

Marsh brushed some cake crumbs off his chest. "Thanks much for the excellent cake. I really do need to be on my way. As always, it's been a real pleasure to trade with you. Dar, you and I will certainly meet again. My travels sometimes take me through Delphi—when I have school supplies for sale!"

Helen helped Clare take the platter inside. "He's not the only person with a schedule. I can reach the Peterson farm before dark if I leave now."

Henry walked with Marsh back to his truck. "Thanks, again."

"My pleasure," the merchant obliged while checking his load and securing the tarp. "I appreciate the business. Hope she gets a lot of use out of those glasses!"

"Why can't you stay?" Dar asked Helen.

The teacher smiled self-consciously in the open doorway. "You're not the only one who can look forward to new and interesting things. I might as well come out with it now. After I finish exams for this year, I'll be working permanently at the school, as one of your teachers…for the next four years."

The engine of Marsh's truck sputtered to life, he put it in gear and drove off.

"That's great!" Dar cheered.

"Yes," Henry agreed as Marsh's truck rolled out of sight.

Helen feigned indignity. "It's about time! I've been waiting for a position to open for nearly five years. My old bones can't take much more of that horse and these roads."

* * *

Marsh drove slowly, with both hands on the wheel, watching his rearview mirror for any hint of sudden movement. He navigated his rattling truck north for five minutes, along bumpy dirt roads, through plowed fields, past the gutted ruins of a large strip mall. Afternoon sun began to sink below the horizon when he drove into the hollow remains of what had been a crash-landed passenger jet.

Decades earlier, salvagers with power tools had claimed the engines, fuel tanks, metal skin, interior fittings, and all the electrical systems. Only the ribbed skeletal carcass remained—the ideal hiding place for an old pickup truck whose driver didn't care to be seen by anyone passing by.

As generous as the Taggert clan was known to be, Marsh knew from past experience that it was always better for him to wait for them. Let them show themselves first, and then get out of the truck. Many of their most notorious henchmen were just a little too eager to beat the aging merchant just for fun.

The sudden flare of a lit match was his cue to get out of his truck and shut the door.

Sorel Taggert stepped in to view. He was taller than Marsh. A black eye patch and several scars on his face said quite a lot to the casual observer about his everyday fearlessness. Dressed in brown camouflage and coated in dust, he let one gloved hand swing free while the other remained stationary on the hilt of a knife on his belt.

"What have you got?" he asked like he didn't care.

Marsh kept his hands plainly visible. "I sure am glad it's you!"

"Nice to be appreciated," Sorel nodded. "Lambert is still on our family's naughty list. What is he up to these days? I can't imagine he'll be happy to see us, even if we are what passes for government in this part of the world."

Marsh got right to the point. "Same as always. Wife and two kids. Son and daughter. Jack is going with Darlene to make sure she gets to school in Delphi without any trouble. They'll be on their way, off the farm, out of your hair. You could just let them go—"

Sorel took one step closer. "Don't tell me how to do my job! Just be glad it's me and not one of the others. My brothers and sisters don't want the same kind of law and order that you do. They cut corners—you know what I mean? So, tell me about the Lamberts, take your money, and go. Let the rest of this unpleasantness take care of itself."

CHAPTER THREE

Very early the next morning, Darlene was in a deep sleep when Jack jostled her awake. "Dad sent me. Get up and get dressed. We got trouble. No lights. Don't make any noise. Just come downstairs when you're ready."

"Okay," she mumbled while struggling to sit up. The digital clock on her nightstand silently displayed 3:35 a.m. as Jack slipped away. His muddy boots thunked on the floor as he went back down to the kitchen.

Dar focused on dressing herself in two warm layers as fast as she could. She cringed when she stepped in some of the mud Jack had carelessly tracked in to her room. "Ew—yuck! Thanks a lot."

Everyone who lived outside the protective walls of a post-Collapse enclave settlement was aware of the risks. Unrestricted civic freedoms and economic prosperity were offset by the dangers of disease, famine, and robbery that so often afflicted anyone who dared to live off the land. As uncommon as they were in settled regions, moments like this were not unheard of in any way. However infrequent, farm families practiced a form of "drill" that allowed them to act swiftly in an emergency.

Knowing what might be at stake, Dar sat on her bed. She laced up both of her boots before putting on a multi-pocket vest. Feeling her way through darkness, she filled each pocket of the vest with her most cherished things, including her old, worn glasses and the recommendation letter that would get her into the Delphi school. Checking the fit of her new glasses, she pulled a stocking cap on to her head before going downstairs.

She was met by the smell of fresh-brewed coffee before she walked in to the kitchen. Three pump shotguns and a trio of leather gun belts bulging with handguns filled the table they would normally gather around for breakfast. Henry, Clare, and Jack were dressed similarly, ready for the cold predawn morning air and trouble.

Her father handed her a steaming cup of coffee. "Couldn't sleep, so I went out early. We've got a large number of fresh horse tracks going in single file all the way around us. They approached from the north, rode all the way around without dismounting. They went back the same way they came in."

Dar drank while Jack reached for a gun belt. Clare gave Dar a piece of buttered toast. "At least six?" she asked while sipping her own coffee.

"Could be more," Henry conceded while draining his mug.

Jack strapped on his favorite pistol. "We haven't been rustled in at least two years," he recalled while checking the fit of his clothing and equipment. "Six guys playing follow the leader want what we have. Why else would they be here?"

"Probably," Henry agreed while putting on his own gun belt. "Let's just stay calm. Everyone knows what they've got to do. We can handle this. Dar, go to the basement and get my bug-out bag; bring it to me. There are some things you and Jack need to know before we stand watch."

Dar ate her toast and drank some coffee.

Clare stepped closer to her husband. "Are you sure?"

Henry nodded. "We agreed to tell 'em when Jack was old enough for high school and we didn't. Are we just going to keep putting it off?"

Clare shrugged. "No. We might as well tell them. I don't think it matters anymore. It just seems unfair to burden them with our past. Most of it happened before they were born. Dar, please do as your father asked and get the bag."

Darlene put her mug on the table and went to the living room with a last bite of toast in her mouth.

Jack picked up a shotgun. "What's the big secret?"

Henry put a reassuring hand on his son's shoulder. "There is an old saying about the road to Hell."

"Paved with good intentions," Jack remembered.

Clare was solemn. "Let's wait until your sister gets back before we open old wounds. I want both of your to understand why some things happened the way they did."

* * *

Dar made her way through the dark living room and into the home's interior hallway, where she opened a door that lead to the basement. Every stair creaked as she descended into the familiar gloom. Alone in the subterranean darkness, she made her way to the nearest shelf. Her probing hands found a row of bloated luggage. Each bag was stuffed with a wide variety of things the family would need in an emergency.

Dar remembered that her father's olive drab half pack was first in line, much heavier than the other haversacks. Using both hands, she slung the heavy load around her neck. Its ponderous weight made her sway back and forth. Dar reached out with both hands to steady herself. She was about to turn around when sounds of gunshots and broken glass erupted overhead. Footfalls and shouting mingled with more gunfire as she scrambled toward the stairs.

The idea that someone was attacking her family inside their house was terrifying! Anger and fear mixed as adrenaline surged through her body. The impulse to fight or flee was powerful. *She had to do something*!

Tearing up the stairs as fast as she could go, Dar was hampered by the weight and bulk of the bag that tugged harshly at her neck with each bounding stride. She flung the door to the interior of the house open with very little hesitation. The boom of several shotgun blasts deafened her as she staggered closer to the firefight.

Dar unsteadily approached the living room. Continuous muzzle flashes blazed from handguns and shotguns. She found herself being partially blinded by the strobe effect and unable to hear over the din. The sudden, indistinct appearance of her mother and father was startling. It was enough to make Dar stop where she was.

The moment was unreal, lasting no more than the blink of an eye. Henry and Clare stood back-to-back in the smoke-filled darkness, each with a bucking shotgun clutched in their rapidly moving hands. Something—or someone—moved nearby, from the direction of the kitchen.

Instinct made Dar scream and back away as the undiscernible opponent was hit by a blast of buckshot at short range. Several stray pellets bounced off a nearby wall. They struck Dar at low velocity on the back of her head and thighs as she fled back down the hallway. Each welt burned as if she'd been touched by hot metal.

Reason gave way to panic as she fled back downstairs, into the very full basement. Clambering through rows of stacked boxes, she rushed to a familiar ground-level window—the same escape route she'd relied on many times as a child when playing hide-and-seek with her brother and the other boys and girls in their neighborhood. Unaware that she had somebody else's blood on her hands, Dar frantically worked the latches until she was forced to wipe the gore on her pants, just to get the feeling of warm slipperiness off her tense fingers.

Cold air hit her in the face when the window flopped open. More shuffling footfalls and shooting upstairs encouraged her to scramble into the open window. The rucksack around her neck was too big. Its coarse, twisting straps mercilessly cut off her breath. Thrashing didn't help.

Dar forced herself to calm down. Wiggling back inside, she removed the pack and shoved it out the window. Gunshots in the house stopped just as she crawled outside, onto the ground that was still wet with morning dew.

Scuttling on shaky hands and knees, Dar leaped to her feet and scooped up the pack. Hugging it close, she ran toward the barn without bothering to see if anyone followed.

Her sudden entry into the barn through a large, squeaking door was enough of a disturbance to motivate the family's slumbering milk cow. Gerry the Guernsey stood up in her stall with a snort that telegraphed just how indignant she was.

Dar pulled the barn door closed. "Don't you dare get snippy with me!" she declared in a loud stage whisper. "We've just been attacked! Mom, Dad, and Jack are in trouble!"

Gerry appeared to take it all in with some doubt. Dar glanced at a small night-light that glowed on the wall nearby. "Did you turn that on? I thought we talked about this!"

The cow shuffled, as if embarrassed.

Dar switched off the light. "We've got to do something!"

She adjusted her glasses before stooping to peek out through a gap in the big hinges that held up the barn door. Dar let the rucksack in her hands fall to the floor.

She took off her knit cap and crammed it into a vest pocket. “Calm down and think.”

Lights were on inside the house. She could see their faint glow through the curtains. Several minutes of nerve-racking silence passed before the domicile’s exterior lighting was turned on.

Dar was relieved. “Must be over,” she concluded.

Gerry’s ears peeled back in a show of bovine worry.

Dar took a deep breath. “Just be cool. Let’s wait and see who comes out. Should be Mom and Dad. I saw them. They were dealing with these guys! Sure hope Jack is OK.”

A muscular, one-eyed man dressed in mottled brown appeared in the doorway to the mudroom at the back of the house. Dar cringed when she saw his eye patch and the smoking shotgun in his hands. He was easy to see in the bright white glow emanating from the house. He paced impatiently back and forth, as if he was mad about something. A shorter, stockier man wearing blue denim came out of the mudroom. The two spoke for several seconds. Dar couldn’t hear what they said to each other.

The one-eyed man pointed at the barn. Dar flinched as the duo began walking toward her hiding place. “Lights out!” she told the cow while scooping up her father’s rucksack. Running to the back of the barn, she hid between two tall stacks of baled hay.

The uncertain Guernsey muttered while moving slowly deeper into her slatted stall.

* * *

Frank followed Sorel Taggert with one hand on his wide gun belt. “Doesn’t matter,” he argued. “They were too well armed. Say what you want about these farmers; they do know to fight!”

Sorel kept a grip on his warm shotgun while Frank opened the barn door. "Anyone would fight for it if they had all of this. Henry got what was coming to him. I'm just sorry we didn't get a chance to talk it over with Clare."

"She would have never come back," Frank gabbed while peering into the depths of the barn. "Sounds like they got a cow in there. Smells like it, too."

Sorel raised his weapon. "Go on. I've got you covered."

Frank took a small flashlight off his gun belt. He turned on the beam with a flick of his wrist. "Yeah," he exhaled when his light found Gerry. "It's a milker. Looks like a good selection of tools, if you're in to that sort of thing."

Sorel glanced over his shoulder. "Get on in there and look around! The others won't be here until after sunrise. We're on our own until then. Might as well make the most of it and get first dibs on the good loot."

Frank shined his light around the interior of the barn. He walked slowly to the back of the structure. "Tools, hay, fence wire, and a back door. Nothing I'd want to claim for my share. All the good stuff is probably in their house. Let's get back inside and search their bodies. They had more than enough guns to make this worthwhile."

Sorel kept the barn door open with the toe of his boot. "Just remember, we have three more farms to roust. That's three more chances for you to end up dead. I should've known Henry Lambert was going to be a tough nut to crack."

Frank lazily turned his back on the uninteresting stacked bales of hay that hid Dar. "What was so special about him?"

"Nothing," Taggert grunted, continuing to scan his surroundings. "You know how my family is about loyalty. Clare was one of us. She had no business going away with him. Not when we could've given them a better life in Tumwater. Coming out here to dig in the dirt like refugees was more than my father could stand."

Frank turned off his flashlight and put it away as he came out of the barn. "Sounds like you had it in for this guy," he speculated while closing the door.

The pair started walking toward the house. Sorel slung his shotgun over his shoulder, "Me? No. I never met him, Clare was an older cousin. I barely knew her when they left our family's protection. Our commitment to law and order is the only thing that has kept this region from being worse than it is. I don't have much say in how we keep the peace. All I can do is my part. Which reminds me, let's have another look for the girl before we start dividing the loot."

"What if she's not here?"

Sorel grimaced. "Like it or not, Seth is in charge now. He'd probably say we have an obligation to run her down and finish what we started so she won't come back later for revenge. If she's not in the house, we ought to start looking when the sun comes up. Her parents and brother got four of us. She'll be a lot harder to catch if she knows that."

Frank snickered.

Sorel slowed and stopped halfway between the house and the barn. "We did what we had to do," he warned. "Expanding the clan's territory is the only way we can get back some of what the Collapse took from us. Nobody follows us unless we give them a reason to. That means some of the carrot or some of the stick when they stray. Just keep your eyes open. Don't let her shoot you in the back."

* * *

Darlene dropped to her knees. She didn't hear everything the one-eyed man said, though it was clear enough from the reaction of his sidekick that her parents were dead. Feelings of anger and hopelessness grew inside her while she watched Sorel and Frank go into her family's cherished abode.

Several seconds passed. She couldn't take her eyes away from a gap in the barn door that gave her an obstructed view of the floodlit house.

All of the perimeter lights around the building went out when somebody inside used a touch screen to turn them off. Dar felt the predawn darkness close in around her as if she was being swallowed by a silent void.

Just a few steps behind the grief-stricken girl, Gerry's fear worsened as the gloom continued. The anxious cow slowly made her way to the reassuring night-light. She turned it on with an audible sigh of relief.

Dar grasped the worn straps of the old haversack between her knees with both hands as the tiny light activated. The sudden brightness galvanized her. "You might be right," she decided. "There's no point just waiting for them to find us. We've got to get away!"

Dar felt defenseless. She wobbled to her feet, realizing that she was unarmed. That helplessness made her want to fling open the barn door and run as fast as she could. Summoning all of her willpower, she succeeded in suppressing the urge to flee in terror.

"No," she declared quietly, reaching out to turn off the night-light. "Stay calm."

Gerry snuffled doubtfully. Dar picked up her father's rucksack, hugging it close. "First thing we do is get out here. The rest can be sorted out later. The way those two were blabbing makes me think there's something going on her we don't know about."

The cow looked indignant.

"Tell me about it," Dar fumed while trying to make up her mind. "Where do we go and who do we tell? You can't talk and who's going to believe me? That one-eyed man said something about expanding Taggert territory and rousting more farms. Lousy, unfair power grab, that's what it is!"

If Gerry couldn't have the night-light, she wanted out of the barn. The agitated cow nudged Darlene impatiently. "Don't rush me!" the teenager complained. "First thing we do is escape, then we go tell somebody who can do something about…whatever this is."

Knowing the people who attacked her family might butcher and eat her beloved cow, Darlene put her burden down to search for a harness. Nimbly feeling her way through the familiar interior of the barn, she rapidly found what she was looking for.

"I know how much you hate this thing," Dar soothed while putting the leather harness around Gerry's ample neck. "We've got to be out of here and miles away before they come back!"

Gerry stood still after she was harnessed. Darlene picked up her haversack just as light glared from the house. She moved slowly to peek through several gaps in a wall.

Sorel and Frank where working together, making a pile of something Dar couldn't see. They came out of the mudroom several times before Dar realized what they were doing. Anger became rage when she realized they were callously dumping bodies on the lawn. Dar squinted in the predawn glow of increasing twilight.

"Can't see if any of them are Mom, Dad, or Jack."

Dar noticed how the darkness was beginning to fade. "We've got less than an hour," she guessed. "It's going to be daylight soon. We've got to go, *now*!"

Frank and Sorel came and went several times. Dar's stomach lurched whenever they dropped whoever they were carrying. The pile of discarded corpses continued to grow. Dar heaved violently when she believed she'd seen her mother on the top of the heap.

She hocked and spit to clear her mouth while wiping away a mournful torrent of tears. More willpower was needed to breathe evenly while she waited for the killers inside the house to turn off the floodlights again.

Dar took a step back to avoid the spreading reek of her vomit. "They're looting our house," she verbalized bitterly. "C'mon, Gerry. We've got to go. Hide and seek."

Dar used the toe of her boot to force open the barn door while guiding the cow into the yard. Gerry followed with some expectation.

As children, Dar and her brother had enjoyed the thrill of hiding behind the bulk of the cow while it sauntered around the farm. Very few people gave Gerry a second thought while she grazed, especially if she didn't appear to be in any distress.

"Hide and seek," Dar repeated confidently while stooping behind the ambling animal. "We're just a hungry cow out for an early morning walk. Nobody else here. Just a cow."

* * *

Frank made his way into the master bedroom. He peeled open the curtains to admire the view of an expansive back yard—and the barn.

Sorel came in several seconds later with a pair of empty saddle bags. "What are you looking at?" he wondered while tossing the bags on to the rumpled bed.

The hired gun turned away from the window. Overhead lighting in the room was bright enough to limit his view of the outside world. "Just wanted to have myself a look. There's no telling when I might get a place like this."

"See anything?"

"Not really," Frank shrugged while reaching for a saddle bag. "Their cow is up and around. Probably wondering why nobody has come to milk it."

Sorel was unconcerned. "Cows are poop machines. That one is probably just hungry. Let's finish going through this place before the others get here. Then, we can worry about having milk or steak for breakfast."

The men worked fast to search for loot, opening every drawer and container they could find.

"Hold on a minute," Sorel said when he was feeling his way through the drapes for any sign of hidden goods. "How many cows put on their own harnesses?"

"What?" Frank said with his hands full of wadded clothing.

Sorel focused his attention on the wandering cow. A glance at his watch confirmed that local sunrise was just minutes away.

"Turn off the light and come over here," he demanded.

Frank dropped what he was doing. He shut off the overhead light and came to stand near Sorel. Looking out through the window, they watched Gerry make her way slowly across the dew-cover lawn. "It's a cow," he concluded sarcastically.

"Wearing a harness," Sorel insisted.

"So?"

"Take a closer look," the one-eyed man sneered. "With or without a harness, how many cows have you ever seen with six legs?"

Frank blinked. "One, two, three, four, five, and six. Yeah, that's the strangest cow I have ever seen. Got to be the kid—their daughter. She doesn't seem to be in a hurry."

Sorel fingered his gun belt while the cow kept moving. "She has enough brains to hide from us. You probably walked right past her in the barn. I'll bet you a fistful of bullets she has a place to go and somebody to ask for help. That's going to be trouble for the clan—if she lives that long!"

Frank turned away from the window. "We've been through most of the upstairs," he observed plainly. "Let's finish the sweep before the others get here. That kid won't be hard to find. We can run her down later."

Sorel watched the cow walk behind a tree and out of his sight. The girl's long legs allowed her to keep up with the disappearing animal's plodding pace. Using the cow for cover was an inspired touch—enough for Sorel to surmise that the Lamberts must have taught their children how to think in a crisis.

Sorel leaned closer to the fogged window for a better look at the corpses in the yard. He wasn't looking forward to what his older siblings would have to say about the death of Clare. "Doesn't matter," he told himself.

Half a dozen mercenaries on horseback were expected to arrive at the Lambert farm just after sunrise, which would give him and Frank more than enough time to claim the best loot for themselves. With their help, Sorel believed he wouldn't have any trouble picking up the girl's trail. All of the surrounding farms were now under the protection of the Taggert clan, whether they wanted to be or not. What's-her-name was an unforeseen problem that would just have to be dealt with.

* * *

Dar guided Gerry away from the house, through the tomato garden her mother liked, onto a gravel path that would take them deep inside acres of tall corn. The load on her back was heavy. "They can't see us now," she decided just as the sun came up. "Let's get out of here. I need time to think and you should be milked."

An hour later, they emerged from the fragrant cornrows on to a muddy dirt track. "Over there," Dar pointed at a distant hill. "Should take no more than fifteen minutes to get there. We can see the Peterson place from there."

Adrenaline faded, causing Dar to shiver with each step through the tall grass that was still slick with morning dew. Fear and uncertainty grew insider her until she reached the top of the familiar foothill and a copse of tall evergreen trees that hid her from casual view. A cluster of rustic buildings was barely visible in the distance. The glistening surface of Black Lake was a silver line on the horizon.

Dar took hold of Gerry by the leather yoke. "See? You remember those people. Let's go and see if they're okay. I'll ask them to look after you, just until we get this worked out."

Gerry looked in the direction of the distant farm, then at Dar.

The cold, wet woman shifted the backpack before it could dig into her shoulders. "I'm going to milk you here. Then, we'll go see the Petersons. As long as you're good and don't run off, it shouldn't take more than two hours to get there."

CHAPTER FOUR

Dar read the time on her digital watch as 8:15 a.m. when she arrived at the Peterson farm. She put the old timepiece back in to a vest pocket, where it wouldn't be lost or scratched. The utter lack of noise from the farm made Dar feel uneasy. "I can hear the livestock," she worried. "Where are the people?"

Helen suddenly appeared as Dar approached the house, her boots crunched through gravel that was scarred by many fresh horse tracks. "Hello, Dar!" she called out while cinching the belt on her customary long, light blue, leather coat, "I'm so glad you're okay," she said with obvious relief, "Where is—"

"They're dead," Dar blurted. "Mom, Dad, and Jack. Taggerts came in the middle of the night and killed them. Where are the Petersons?"

Helen brushed at her unkempt hair. She gestured at the rustic post-Collapse house. "Please, stay outside. The Petersons are okay. They've just been worked over by the Taggerts and their goons."

Dar laid a hand on the docile cow standing next to her. "What's going on?"

Helen came closer. "The worst was over before I got here," she blustered. "Ben Taggert rode with a posse to say this area is now under their family's protection."

Dar was shocked and outraged. "Why would they do that?"

The teacher was blunt. "The word is extortion. Just do what the Taggerts tell you to do and nobody gets hurt. The Petersons are inside and they're okay. Yes, even the kids. They're all embarrassed, but otherwise unharmed."

Dar's heart sank while she stroked the back of Gerry's neck. "Does anyone know why this is happening?"

Helen's expression darkened. "They—the Taggerts—are expanding their territory. They've been the heavy hand in this region since the Collapse. It all started with their ancestors, who were career politicians in the city of Tumwater, decades before things went wrong. In the last twenty years or so, they've taken it upon themselves to impose their version of law and order on this region."

Dar was incredulous. "The Petersons are going along with this?"

"They are," Helen confirmed, looking over her shoulder.

In the house behind her, curtains moved from several windows to reveal fearful faces.

"The Taggerts are a very large family," she explained. "I'm sorry to tell you that they've done this kind of thing before. Matriarch or patriarch—whoever is ruthless enough to be in charge of that menagerie—they give orders to their adult sons and daughters that are allegedly based on old laws that nobody remembers. Their so-called 'job' is to go out in all directions and break the bad news. Anyone who won't be loyal to them gets worked over by their hired muscle."

Dar's face reddened. Tears flowed. "Why did they—"

Helen hugged the devastated adolescent. "I am so sorry!" she consoled intensely with tears of her own. "It's a terrible thing. It wasn't just your mother; your father also had history with those people."

"I don't understand," Dar breathed through her pain, "What are you talking about?"

Helen released her embrace. Both of them took a moment to wipe away their tears. "Like many other people, your parents chose to live out here, far away from the Taggerts and their way of doing things. You can think of it as a form of insult that the Taggerts wouldn't allow themselves to forgive or forget."

"Why not?"

Helen slumped. "It's just not in their nature to tolerate resistance. Once upon a time, one of them was the mayor of that city—elected to the office or born to serve. Depends on who you ask. They probably meant well, especially when the laws became harsher. Before you ask, the answer is no. I'm not that old. I wasn't around for the worst of it. All I've seen is what brought us to…this."

Dar swayed with dismay. Large and small fragments of suddenly relevant nostalgia flared, flickered, and faded in her anguished mind. "I never did give it much thought," she conceded while pulling herself together. "They were just a bunch of old stories. I should have paid more attention!"

"No," Helen counseled. "That's not it. Your parents wanted you and your brother to have a clean slate. They were hoping the influence of the Taggerts wouldn't reach this far. Not for a long time."

Dar sniffled. "Looks like the past caught up with us. What am I supposed to do?"

The older woman looked around apprehensively. A sudden surge of noise from the faraway chicken coop was drowned out by the sound of squealing of pigs. "I think we're about to have company."

Dar cringed when she got a glimpse of Sorel Taggert on horseback, cantering around the side of the house. He came into full view, brandishing a big semiautomatic pistol in his hand. He was followed by five riders. Each of them was armed with rifle or shotgun.

She leaned closer. "Wolf!" she yelled in to the cow's curled ear. "Wolf, wolf, wolf!"

Gerry knew what *that* word meant. She bellowed in mortal fear, bolting away from the approaching horsemen.

"That is a seriously fast cow," one of Taggert's trailing riders commented.

Helen took one long step away from Dar, toward Sorel and his cohorts. "Stop!"

Sorel halted his horse while holstering his gun. His subordinates came to a halt behind him before spreading out to his left and right. Following their leader's example, they kept their hands away from their firearms.

Helen sternly glared at the uneven line of armed ruffians arrayed in front of her. "Sorel Taggert, you have no business here! Your kin have already been here and gone. Looks like you got your way with these people, so move along!"

The one-eyed man was resolute. "Helen, we really don't want any trouble with you."

Dar's fear began to melt. She turned to watch Gerry gallop out of sight. Knowing that link to the past was safe, she focused her attention on the Taggert problem.

The teacher remained defiant. "Darlene Lambert is my student!"

Sorel became fierce. "Come on, now. You know how things are done. That girl—"

"Is a witness to your crimes!" Helen yelled loud enough for the sheltered Peterson family to hear inside their house. "Look," she said with a bit more tact, "just go away and let me take her off to school. She can't hurt you!"

Sorel shook his disheveled head. "Sorry, can't do it. I wish we could just make a place for her and call it good. We've all seen enough today to know that's not possible. I'd never hear the end of it. Might not even live long enough to learn from the mistake if I just let her go. That's just what it'd be—my fault—when she comes back for revenge."

"Some people might call that justice."

"They might," he admitted with a slow nod. "Let's just agree to disagree about that. It's your job to teach and it's my job to make sure that all the old hatchets stay buried. I'm sorry for the mess. I really am. Take a sec and do the math. You'll see. The numbers are on my side. My six beats your two."

Dar was speechless.

Helen widened her stance. "I do remember that you were good at math," she recalled stoically, resting both hands on the belt of her long blue coat. "Henry and Clare had their own reasons for coming out here, which amounted to getting away from people like you. Doesn't that make their kids blameless?"

"My six still beats your two," Sorel insisted heartlessly.

Helen unleashed her belt, the folds of her coat fell open to reveal her pair of six-guns. "There are six of you and I have twelve bullets. The first one of you who moves gets to find out how good my aim is!"

Faces vanished from each window of the Peterson house as the family fled for cover.

Sorel raised one hand to put off the massacre. "Everybody stop!" he warned as loud as he could. "You know the order! Nobody harms Helen!"

Darlene felt vulnerable. "Please, don't—"

Helen raised her voice. "Dar, please. You're interrupting a delicate negotiation."

Dar fought back tears. "Don't do this! I don't want—"

"It's not about what you want, kid!" Sorel spat.

Helen called out with all the bravado she could muster. "Hey! I'm the one with the most bullets! Don't look at her. Everyone keep your eyes on *me*!"

Helen took a sudden step forward while she pulled her guns. A quick flick of each wrist cocked the revolvers. She pointed them at the mounted men arrayed in front of her. "Do I have your attention?"

"Yes, ma'am," he conceded reluctantly without looking directly down the gun barrels.

Helen slowly moved backwards to stand near Darlene. She didn't take her eyes off Taggert and his men. "Leave, *now*! Get away from here as fast as you can!"

"Where do I go?" Dar gulped.

Helen deliberately moved to shield Dar with her body. She stood doggedly between the girl and the raiders. Sorel eyed every move she made. "I can't stop them from following you, but we can all stay here for a while—until the next Taggert and his posse comes to visit. I don't care how you get to Delphi. Just go to the school. *Now*!"

"What about you?"

The older woman remained self-assured. The big revolvers in her hands barely moved. "Dar, listen. The Taggerts have always gone out of their way to leave me alone because I teach their children. I showed half the kids around here how to read, write, and do math. That probably includes some of these knuckleheads. They're all so hairy and dirty, it's hard to tell who is who!"

The conflicted teenager thought she understood that Helen had her own unique place in the harsh community of post-Collapse factions that were competing for dominance. Her only hope was to reach safety—a place where the Taggerts couldn't easily harm her. The school made sense. It was far away, and full of students and adults the ruling family couldn't justify hurting—even if they wanted to!

Watching the armed men on horseback she could see, Dar realized that none of this was personal for them. They were doing what the one-eyed man told them to do. Sorel appeared to be following the orders given by an older member of his family.

"Lousy politics," she decided.

"Maybe so," Helen asserted severely. "That doesn't change what's happening here. You need to get moving! I'll make sure you have a head start. That's the best I can do. Please believe me when I say that somebody named Taggert will be hot on your trail before the sun goes down. Don't stop for anything. Don't trust anyone!"

"Believe what she says," Sorel intoned vindictively from the saddle of his horse. "It's not going to change anything, but it is good advice. We have lots of friends everywhere. That's how we keep the peace. We are always going to know where you are!"

Helen didn't waver. "Don't stop for anything. Don't trust anyone. *Go*."

* * *

Dar didn't remember turning to run. In the blink of an eye, she was loping through knee-high grass, toward the distant, gleaming waters of Black Lake. Urgency propelled her aching legs. Her lungs burned. She perspired heavily with the passing of each minute. Four and a half grueling miles rolled by under her frantic feet, until exhaustion forced her to slow and stop to catch a ragged breath.

The fragrant green needles of a tall black spruce tree provided her with some shade while she wheezed. Scattered cloud cover gave way to blue sky and sunshine before she recovered enough vigor to take stock of her bleak situation and figure out where she was. The familiar glistening surface of Black Lake was no long as visible as it had earlier been.

"I'm closer," she concluded after spitting out loose phlegm.

Dar leaned on the tree that sheltered her. She adjusted her glasses before searching the horizon in all directions. The house and barn of another family-run farm was visible near what she believed was the shoreline of the lake.

Knowing that the Taggert clan was exerting their influence on everyone in the area, Dar understood why she needed to stay away from those people. They were just doing what they had to in a bad situation.

She pulled off her sweat-soaked stocking cap. Wiping her face dry, she thought about her next move. Should she steal a boat and make her way south, along the length of Black Lake, to a point near Delphi, or would it be safer to sneak through farm country until she reached Belmore? Fears of being shot as a thief or drowning in the lake—especially at night—motivated her to remain on dry land until she could find some way into the enclave.

Dar put the damp hat in a vest pocket. Working her way around the nearby homestead, she used the sun as a reference to keep going in a southerly direction. Old memories came back while she walked.

Dar's parent's had taken her and her younger brother to Belmore twice in the past ten years. On both of those occasions, they travelled in a borrowed horse-drawn wagon full of root vegetables harvested from the family's land.

Hot midday sun beat down on her as Dar tried to remember the route that Jack was supposed to escort her on to reach the school in Delphi. They'd spent weeks planning every step of what should have been a casual journey. They'd camp outdoors to avoid calling attention to themselves—or the large sum of money they'd be carrying to pay for Dar's first year of high school.

The afternoon sun began to descend as Dar pushed through several cornfields. She stopped to drink from a creek that seemed familiar, one of many she remembered from a simple map Jack had drawn by hand. Banishing her thirst made Dar think of food. She sat in the shade of an apple tree, within sight of an uneven dusty north-south road that should lead her to Belmore.

Dar had always thought she knew what was in everyone's bug-out bags. They'd been packed and unpacked so many times that she stopped noticing what her parents put in them. That inattentiveness caused her to be surprised when she opened her father's rucksack. Pulling the zipper and peeling the pack open, she found more than she expected.

Dar was momentarily stunned when her gaze fell on a beat-up semiautomatic pistol. The handgun rested snugly in a black synthetic holster that could be attached to her vest or worn as a shoulder rig.

She flinched as her fingertips brushed the surface of the gun. She couldn't help feeling guilty about the unfair, violent deaths of Henry, Clare, and Jack. Her frustration at her inability to do something—*anything*—boiled over into a spasm of tears that left her numb and weeping for several minutes.

Unaware that she was impulsively clawing her way through the content of the bag, Dar took a deep breath when her probing hands found the box of bullets and three clips. A fat pile of crumpled papers fell into her lap, releasing a clattering stack of gold coins on the ground between her legs. Losing control of all that cash made her stop thinking about the handgun. Dar let the pistol drop. She rapidly scooped up the money, hiding it deep inside her multi-pocket vest.

Like most people her age, Dar was familiar with currency as a medium of exchange. Until that breathtaking moment, she'd only seen a United States double-eagle gold coin in the textbooks that Helen had loaned her for her studies. Now, she had a whole dozen of them jingling in her pockets!

Reality intruded when Dar heard a slowly approaching horse and two-wheeled wagon on the road. She scrambled to gather her things and hide in the nearby bushes before the driver was close enough to see her. Folded papers fell from her grasp while she fumbled with the holster. Sticky tabs easily fastened it to her vest in a way that was comfortable.

She snugged the gun into place with short-lived satisfaction. Voices on the road got her attention. Somebody was talking to the wagon driver!

Stooping to pick up the fallen pages, she peeked through the foliage that concealed her. The horse and cart she'd heard earlier were now stopped. The driver was chatting with two men on horseback. She recognized one of them immediately. A fellow dressed in blue denim was much dirtier than when she'd watched him desecrate her family's home in the early morning hours.

Dar diverted her gaze to finish gathering the scattered pages and stuff them into her rucksack. Candy bars and beef jerky were briefly visible before she hurriedly mashed everything in. The sound made by the zipper when she closed it was frighteningly loud. She looked back at her pursuers, who were still talking. They were too far away to hear what little noise she was making in the bushes.

Acutely aware of her vulnerability, Dar threw the pack over one shoulder. She turned around in a search for the easiest way to leave the area without being seen from the road. Using both hands to quietly push branches out of her way, she fled without realizing she had dropped one of the old, yellowed pages.

CHAPTER FIVE

Late afternoon sun painted the sky fiery red-orange as Sorel Taggert dismounted from his panting horse with a bounce. He was greeted by a series of waves from men and women mingling near a cluster of bushes at the side of the road.

"What was so important?"

Frank emerged from the crowd. "She's definitely going this way." He pointed in the southerly direction of Belmore. "Everyone we spoke to had no idea she was in the area, then—" he held up a folded pieced of very old paper. "Yeah, well. We found this. In the bushes, over there."

Sorel was unimpressed. "So, she's a litterbug. What about it?"

Frank handed over the find. "Go ahead, read it."

The tired man shook off some of his fatigue. He gently unfolded what looked like an official document. Sorel turned it toward the setting sun, holding it at arm's length to make small print come into focus. His jaw dropped.

"See what I mean?" Frank prodded.

Sorel was in his mid-thirties. He no longer believed any of the stories people still told about Haven. Even if there had been a sanctuary that was capable of taking in all comers, it must be long gone by now. Any one location with that much food, water, and medicine would've been hard-pressed to defend all that loot. Like most cynics, Sorel attributed the power of that persistent myth to the false hope of people who had nothing else to live for.

"Well?"

Sorel was unable to control his astonishment. "Frank, do you know what this is?"

The illiterate ruffian stammered. "I know it's got the word 'haven' on it, h-a-v-e-n. Everyone here has seen that much. We may not have your education, but we do know what print writing looks like. That's official, whatever it is."

The incredulous man held the page a little higher in the fading light for a second look. "That *is* official," he decided after several seconds of tortured study. "First of two pages. No way to know what's on the second page without seeing it. Washington State National Guard. Says here, it's an evacuation order for Zone 26 of Thurston Country. That's what this area used to be. 'Residents are advised to make their way to Haven Site Seven-Six-Eight-Five. If you have questions or need directions, please consult your online social services portal.' I have no idea what that means."

Frank wasn't sure if he should be encouraged or disappointed. He glanced sidelong at the surly crowd of would-be scavengers hungrily watching their every move. "That is, for sure, a lot of words." He grinned nervously. "Before you got here, the bunch of us were hoping there was more to it. You follow me?"

As shocked as he was, Sorel did get the point. The only thing more exaggerated than Haven mythology was the lurid gossip about people who went looking for places like it. Anyone who couldn't pony up some piece of hard-to-explain loot was a liar. Those who could show off something rare were still hard to believe. Real or not, most of them had one thing in common—they all jabbered ceaselessly about their hardships and the horrors that mercilessly stalked them in dark, scary places.

Sorel made a show of carefully folding the page and putting it in his shirt pocket. "Everybody calm down. This might not be anything more than some old piece of trash. Stop and think. Why does the Lambert kid have this? She might not even know what it is. Stay cool and let me figure this out. Anyone who goes running off to search for treasure loses this week's pay!"

* * *

Heat, thirst, and hunger slowly drained Darlene's vigor as she walked. Avoiding the more well-travelled southbound road that would easily direct her to the Belmore enclave, she meandered through the maze of dry irrigation ditches and narrow access roads that crisscrossed the countryside. She bypassed broken concrete chunks and jagged portions of rusting metal girders without any interest in how that pre-Collapse debris got there.

Her fog-filled memory nauseously acknowledged what her parents and grandparents had called "the great dismantling." Roads, homes, and businesses had all been removed to make room for life-sustaining agriculture. So many of the same stories had been told so many times that very few people openly questioned what they were told about those desperate days and what it took to survive them—not anymore. It was enough just to be grateful for the sacrifices of those who somehow lived long enough to reclaim the land.

Dar staggered to a halt near the open end of a broken pipe sticking out of the ground. A clear stream of water trickled out of it. Knowing the water could somehow be tainted, she knelt and drank, using both hands to cup the invigorating moisture to her dry mouth. Instinct overcame reason; she drank until she was satisfied.

Still on her knees, Dar opened her pack to search for something to put water in. She found an empty plastic bottle in the depths of the rucksack and filled it. Screwing the lid back on to the scarred clear bottle, she held it with one hand for several seconds while her thoughts coalesced.

Stowing the bottle, she put one of the high-calorie candy bars in a vest pocket before closing and shouldering the pack. Unwrapping the sweet treat was a mindless act, performed while she made her way around tree stumps into a shaded area that was encircled by ubiquitous apple trees. Selecting a semi-ripe apple from a low-hanging leafy branch, she sat to eat. The darkening crimson sky was of no concern while she gobbled the apple, slowing only to nibble the candy bar. It wasn't the kind of hearty meal she was used to, though every bite of it tasted extraordinarily good.

As disoriented as Dar knew she must be, she felt certain that Belmore was nearby. Located within five miles of Tumwater, the community was a patchwork of workshops and farms that did brisk business with a loose association of self-made entrepreneurs. Darlene remembered that Marsh, the travelling merchant, owned a shop or a warehouse inside the protective walls of the enclave. How hard would it be for her to find him?

She quietly considered the problem. It was common knowledge that approaching any settlement after dark on foot was a bad idea. With or without a source of light, she was likely to be hurt by fearful sentries who had orders to shoot first and ask questions later. That grim certainty made the weight of the small flashlight that was clipped to her vest feel unimportant. Uneasiness was enough to inspire curiosity. She put the now-dirty pack on her lap and started going through it.

Repositioning her glasses, she brushed matted hair out of her face. The remaining candy bars slid through her fingers, their slick bright wrappers glowing in the setting sun. As old as those synthetic candies were known to be, the one she'd eaten tasted like it had been recently made. She'd known families who were wealthy enough to own and use food fabricators. The delicacies they served were mind-blowing.

Finding a can of what the label said was cod soup, she eyed the pull top suspiciously. "How can anything so old still be safe to eat?"

The box of bullets and three empty clips for the pistol were put aside while Dar dug further into the bag. The folded stack of paper was now crumpled into an uneven wad. She pulled the pages apart, making some effort to flatten out the creases. Each page was a mechanically printed form of some kind. Dar's heart skipped a beat when she realized that two of them were birth certificates—one each for herself and her brother Jack.

Rifling through the remaining pages, she was surprised to discover a marriage license and a land deed; the names of her parents were featured prominently on both documents. Seeing her mother's lengthy full name spelled out was jarring. Dar read out loud softly, "Clare Louise Taggert-Lambert."

She laughed when she realized her father's middle name was Donald. The giggle was enough to fend off a sudden attack of melancholy. "Not any worse than mine or Jack's," she told herself. The next form to be unfolded was a military document full of numbers, in the name of Henry C. Lambert. Darlene knew he had been her grandfather. At the bottom of the page, in big red letters, she read: Honorable Discharge; Authorized for Haven Site access, Thurston County, Washington, Register Location 7685. Admit recipient and spouse, Elizabeth C. Taggert Lambert."

"Grandma and Grandpa," she realized.

As much as she'd loved her grandparents, her brother Jack had always paid more attention to their obviously embellished stories about hordes of rampaging robots and chaotic city evacuations. Grandpa Lambert's reticence on the subject of his or anyone else's military service had never mattered to her until now. Grandma Liz didn't say much more, though she did joke about it—enough to keep Jack in stitches!

Dar's roaming eye came back to her grandmother's name. "Taggert," she muttered. "I didn't know that. I guess you guys are a pain in the neck for everybody. Wonder why my parents never thought this was important?"

She took her glasses off, squinting at the page to be sure she was reading it properly. "Haven Site access," she mumbled in disbelief. "I know my family has lived here for a long time. You'd think they'd be proud of something like—um—whatever this is."

The last piece of aging paper to receive her attention appeared to be the second half of a two-part document. She put her glasses on. "Page two of two," she read succinctly. "Warning. This is a temporary evacuation. Please do not bring anything you don't need. Only bare essentials. Household pets are permitted. Robots or androids must be preregistered and quarantined. Medical assistants only—including mobile fabrication systems—with a doctor's approval. The following items and products are not permitted inside the boundaries of Haven Sites."

The rest of the page meant nothing to her—three columns of shorthand descriptions for things she could only guess about. "No firearms," she observed dryly after a second read. "No gauss weapons. No energy weapons. Yeah, I'll have to leave those with a friend."

As intriguing as the implications were, Dar neatly folded the gathered pages and put them in one of her already full vest pockets. Chewing beef jerky, she found and repacked three freeze-dried meals; two pairs of dry socks; a jar of ointment; a rolled up bandage; a ball of string; a stiff roll of rough toilet paper; a large, warm, red blanket labeled E-M-S; and a small, sleek, black metal gadget.

Dar held the last object in the palm of her hand, starring at a slowly turning illuminated arrow on the face of whatever it was. Just having it felt strange. It seemed out of place.

Both of her parents had always been careful about what they put in their survival gear. Everyone—all four of them—had a compass in their vest. Why would her father have another one put away? Her overactive imagination conjured a facsimile of Helen's voice. "The word you're looking for is 'redundant,' meaning in addition to."

She scowled. "This is nothing more than an extra compass. What else could it be?"

Dar noticed a button on the gadget labelled "seek." Pressing it made the simulated needle on the display turn in a westerly direction. "Whatever that means," she grunted.

She put the curiosity back in to the rucksack. Looking skyward for several seconds, she decided that sunset and full darkness would be upon her within three or four hours. That would give her enough time to find a place to sleep for the night.

Dar stood with a groan, slowly turning in place to be certain that she wasn't going to leave anything on the ground.

She thought about Helen while zipping the rucksack and putting it over her aching shoulder. Most of her living memory included frequent visits from the travelling teacher. Most of them ended with some sort of exam, followed by an evening meal shared with the rest of her family. Dar and Jack usually studied at the same time—always in the kitchen, after the last of the day's chores were done.

She walked down a dirt track for several minutes, allowing herself to be nostalgic about the ways in which they used to so casually cooperate. Sharing books and pencils with Jack was never hard; he wasn't selfish very often.

Slipping through a large, wide thorn bush made her think about the few fights they'd had over the years. They had always been about privacy or personal space. Prowling down the length of a rusty chain-link fence in search of an opening, she was once more forced to hold back tears of regret when feelings of loss threatened to overwhelm her.

Shortly after darkness fell, Dar squirmed down an embankment, into a rain ditch. Using her small flashlight, she carefully found her way underground, into what remained of an old residential basement. The aboveground structure was long gone, though its foundation and plumbing remained. As a child, she'd found and explored many such places within a five-mile radius of her family's farm.

Dar took off her new glasses and put them away. She wrapped herself in the EMS blanket to keep insects from crawling over the length of her body. Nestling in to the desiccated remains of weeds and leaves, she slept restlessly.

Tormented by a fragmented series of nightmares, she re-experienced the massacre of her family over and over again, until fatigue forced her to sleep deeply enough to stop the dreams from happening. The last thing she remembered before exhaustion overwhelmed her was Helen's bravado—feet planted, arms raised, guns pointed, without any hesitation.

Dar woke at the crack of dawn. The old habit made it possible for her to freshen up, feed herself, and start walking before most farmhands began their work in the fields. She made her way back to the north-south road, mingling with dozens of men and women on their way into the Belmore enclave. Few of them spoke. Many of them yawned. All of them walked casually. Dar cleaned her glasses with a handkerchief when she got close enough to see rusting railroad tracks running parallel to the road.

The residents of Belmore were still proud of their community's transportation history. They put some effort into maintaining infrequent train service between their settlement and the nearby city of Tumwater. That maintenance included every serviceable connecting portion of track within a radius of the industrious enclave—northward, toward Olympia; southward, to Tenino, where the Centralia settlements overlapped.

Approaching Belmore's western gate, Dar walked through narrow, winding streets past dozens of ramshackle buildings. She loitered close enough to the fortified gate to see a spray-painted sign that read; *No Guns*. That post-Collapse prohibition was common to most enclaves when they encouraged their own badged officers to enforce the law. Dar felt the weight of the pistol under her arm. It reminded her that she wasn't safe.

The sound of an approaching train made her recall something Helen had once told her about rail service westward, to Delphi. Dar watched the guards at the gate do their job while she waited for the train to get closer. They were dressed in threadbare municipal uniforms, wearing Belmore Police Department badges, most of which were post-Collapse reproductions. Several hundred yards away, she could see what appeared to be a train station and a trading post.

A trio of air horns blared from the cab of the decelerating locomotive when it was within a mile of the enclave. Dar walked toward the raised platform where the train would stop, as if she was just another potential passenger.

Increasing apprehensiveness on her part and a physical commotion at the gate made Dar curious enough to stop and look. Six very bossy, well-equipped men with automatic weapons pushed their way through several lines of people waiting to enter the enclave. Dar couldn't help noticing they were all similarly dressed. It was common knowledge that Taggert-backed police formations often had better uniforms and more equipment. The formidable image they projected was politically advantageous to the Taggert family. Most of the smaller enclaves in the vicinity of Tumwater asked for, grudgingly accepted, or hesitantly tolerated the presence of those enforcers. As heavy-handed as they were, their effectiveness couldn't be denied.

One of them pointed at the oncoming train. "There it is!" he shouted, "Get closer!"

Dar took a few steps closer to the nearest onlooker. "What's that all about?"

An older man in stained work clothes tugged on his sagging tool belt. "Taggert men," he complained without much interest in the person who was questioning him. "They act like that train belongs to them. It doesn't!"

"Are they…looking for someone?"

"Might be," the mechanic agreed, "Maybe. You know how it is, one thing or another.

"Does the train go to Delphi?"

"It certainly does," he exhaled while keeping an eye on the hubbub. "Every ten days or so, depending. The next run to Delphi is tomorrow, if you're interested."

"Thanks," Dar acknowledged before walking away.

Feelings of unjust persecution began to grow with each step through the morning mud. She genuinely believed they were looking for her—or anyone else who might question their authority.

"Must be a long list," she decided bitterly.

Turning her back on the noisily advancing guards, Dar wormed her way through the crowd toward a scattered cluster of flimsy shacks. Like most thriving enclaves, Belmore put up with anyone who lived or worked outside their built-up earthen walls, as long as they did so without making trouble for the wealthier residents.

"Good luck finding me in there!"

Improvised structures like those she was approaching encircled established enclaves everywhere. They formed a maze of passageways and twisting alleys that were just large enough for people and too small for automobiles. Dar pretended to know where she was going. Five minutes later, she found a vacant overhang near an empty room full of trash. Just enough solitude to sit and think about her next move without being robbed—or worse!

CHAPTER SIX

The overworked train pulled out at precisely 8 a.m. Sorel Taggert watched it go from the saddle of his horse. Behind him, a trio of burly men with rifles waited silently. Seconds later, Ben Taggert and six of his trusted people arrived on horseback. He was followed closely by Belmore's senior law enforcement officer, who was also accompanied by three men and two women he could trust.

"Still playing with trains?" Ben joked with his brother while getting off his horse.

Sorel glanced at the clear, blue sky before stepping off his mount. "She wasn't on it. Doesn't surprise me. If we move fast enough, we can get ahead of her. Stop her from reaching that school and it's over."

Ben waited for the others to dismount. He turned toward the arriving police officers. "This is Captain Drake," he indicated with a sweep of his hand. "It's better if we talk to him now, before this goes any further."

Sorel knew what unspoken rebuke sounded like, especially when it came from family. "Captain," he nodded mechanically, "I think we have a runner—"

Drake looked right at Sorel while touching the gold braided brim of his peaked cap to emphasize his authority. "Good morning, Sorel. Let's cut through it and get to the point. Ben has already heard what I'm about to tell you. My orders are from the town council. Everyone around here has heard about recent events in Tumwater. We know all about your new leadership. I'm sorry for your loss, but that doesn't change anything for us. We're still not going to clean up your mess."

Sorel watched Ben's reaction before he spoke. "All we're asking for is cooperation."

Drake was unmoved. "The answer is *no*," he affirmed emotionlessly. "I don't care if she *is* here. As long as she doesn't break any of our laws—"

Ben put a hand on Sorel. "Let's not get carried away," he soothed. "We're just trying to fix a misunderstanding. The young lady has the wrong idea. All we want now is a few minutes of her time, to explain our situation."

Drake was in his mid-fifties. He came from a long line of career police officers that could trace their history back to the Second World War. He had no illusions about who or what he was dealing with. As diplomatic as Benjamin Taggert tried to be, he was still just another post-Collapse predator who was trying to tie up an inconvenient loose end. Experience had taught him that, however it had happened, Darlene Lambert's only crime was surviving the Taggerts' brutality.

Careful to keep both of his hands away from his gun belt, he gestured at the enclave. "None of you is the mayor of this place. Our elections are honest and we don't use pre-Collapse bureaucratic tricks to stay in power. If she's here, she's our responsibility!"

Ben gripped Sorel's shoulder. "Stay cool," he warned everyone within earshot. "We'll just walk around and have a look."

Sorel glared angrily at his older brother.

Drake pointed at the nearby guarded gate. "I want all of your people outside our walls within the hour."

Sorel's anger boiled over. "Are you sure that's a good idea?"

Drake could feel the officers behind become more agitated. "This isn't Tumwater," he said for their benefit. To mollify them, he continued, "Both of you can tell your new head honcho that I said so. You might have enough muscle to reach out this far. That doesn't mean you'll keep what you try to take."

Ben was cautiously indignant. Seizing a handful of homesteads was one thing; acquiring the allegiance of an entire enclave was something else. That logistical factoid made this cop dangerous. "Times change, Captain Drake. Our father had his own way of doing things. He's gone now. That does make room for—"

"Can it," Drake interrupted. "Whatever you think is happening here, it's not!"

"We'll go," Ben assured while nudging Sorel. "You've clearly got your problems and we've got ours. One of us will be back. Don't be surprised if we have a need to remind you about this lack of respect."

Drake turned to his officers. "Until she breaks a law, this girl is just another visitor!" He said nothing about his worst fear—the possibility that Dar would want to swear out a complaint against the Taggerts for murder.

"One thing at a time," he said rhetorically. "Anyone who has a problem with these fellas, bring it to me!"

"We will be seeing you," Ben vowed sinisterly while the officers got on their horses.

Captain Drake turned his mount away from the train station. "Protect and serve. Look it up. You might learn something."

Sorel waited for the Belmore cops to be on their way. "Have you had a chance to look at the piece of paper we found?"

Ben shrugged. "It's not much to go on."

Sorel leaned in close to whisper. "People in my crew are talking."

"Mine too," Ben confided. "Never hurts to have a goal. Let 'em gossip. This Haven thing makes them greedy. They'll work just a little harder looking for the girl."

Sorel began to doubt his own avarice. "You don't think there's anything to it?"

Ben was practical. "They believe it," he said without raising his voice or pointing at any of the underlings around them. "Think of it as a form of motivation. Let's use that to our advantage. Keep your mouth shut about Haven. Make them focus on the task at hand. The girl knows something or she doesn't."

Sorel grinned with sudden inspiration. "I can think of one way to find out what she knows about Hav—you know, the place. She's got no family and only one place to go where she'll be welcome. We get between her and that school, she'll have to improvise. If she's scared or desperate enough, she'd lead us right to it."

Ben smiled. "It's nice to know your fat head is good for more than wearing a hat. Draw supplies for three days. Take five guns with you and get a move on! Go to Delphi and wait for me to get there. I'll finish things here. It'll take me the rest of the day just to be sure she's not in the enclave or someplace nearby. There's a lot of shacks out here. More than enough alleys for her to hide in. I'll spread some money around and see what our sources can tell us."

* * *

Dar was alone with her thoughts for several morose minutes. The surrounding gloom of the trash-filled room increased her feeling of inadequacy. The stink assaulting her nose seemed strangely appropriate.

"I'm not helpless," she told herself half-heartedly.

She did know that she needed a plan. As defeated as she felt, there were still choices to be made. Escape was somehow just not enough; survival had to have more meaning than that—didn't it? Something her parents and grandparents had said many times came back to her.

"We make the future we want to live in," she whispered.

What had been easily ignored homespun wisdom was now suddenly quite important. Dar sat on a broken piece of furniture, hugging her father's rucksack. Nostalgia faded as understanding bloomed in her mind.

"Okay," she asserted out loud. "They're all gone. It's up to me. I'm not the cause of this. I didn't do anything that made this happen, but I do have to live with it."

She reconsidered the pack in her lap. "I am going to live. It's the right thing to do. I've got what I need to start over. Even if I didn't, I'd still have the obligation to try."

Hearing her own words echo off the moldy walls, she stood up and looked around. "I'm talking to myself in a dark, dirty room filled with garbage that smells like a toilet. This is not a good start."

A distant reverberating blare of air horns gave notice that the train was leaving. Dar slung the pack over her shoulder. She peeked out of her hiding place before stepping into the alley. Walking with a new sense of purpose, she passed a dozen people who were going the other way. Finding her way back out into the open air, she took a deep breath and wiped her nose. Throngs of people dressed like she was moved around her. She was startled to realize that she was blending in.

She approached the enclave's official trading post surrounded by men and women wearing muddy boots and scroungy backpacks. Some had well-worn hats; others did not. She was surprised to see there was a long line of patrons queuing to enter the trading post. Curious to see what might be for sale, she got in line.

Waiting soon became monotonous. Dar observed the people in front and behind her for subtle clues about her surroundings. People who apparently hadn't met before quickly discovered they had things in common. Their demeanor was casual. Most, if not all, of them chatted cheerfully with each other about nothing that mattered.

Briefly experiencing something that felt like anonymity had a calming effect on Dar. She didn't feel quite so persecuted. It wasn't tranquility, but it was enough to reduce the urge to cry.

Feeling less like a victim and more like the determined survivor she was, Dar soaked up the sights and sounds of everyday life in Belmore until it was her turn to approach the trading post. Fugitive or not, she needed the kind of supplies that would enable her to avoid being captured or killed.

As she neared the front of the line, Dar was able to more clearly see the entrance to the trading post. This mercantile was no different than the sort of shop anyone might encounter in a post-Collapse community. Fortified against attack, it was deliberately built outside the walls that protected the enclave's most important resources and residents from the ravages of crime and desperation. Anyone who was not allowed to come and go from the interior of the enclave was limited to whom or what they could do business with on the outside, in the rough, semi-lawless areas near the walls.

Dar was hard-pressed to recall anything useful about this trading post, even though she had been here before when she was much younger. Struggling to remember motivated her to examine the building for details that might jog her memory. That's when she saw someone she did remember—a disheveled man dressed in dirty denim wearing a gun belt.

"Oh, no!"

Fear and rage mingled to heighten her irate senses. Dar stood up straight and balled her fists. She looked left and right to see if the killer was alone. He seemed to be bored, or perhaps waiting for something. He did glance briefly at each person who went through the reinforced door to the trading post. "You're looking for me," she dreaded quietly.

Dar continued to evaluate the uninterested man with smoldering rage while the line of patrons moved closer to him and the doorway of the shop. She was surprised to see him look right at her, then away at someone or something else. A jolt of adrenaline made her flinch when she realized—*he didn't recognize her!*

Time stood painfully still for several terrifying seconds as Dar forced herself to think. The urge to run away competed subconsciously with the need for life-sustaining supplies. Asserting her willpower, she moved one hand slowly up to her face. The man in denim looked right at her when she adjusted her glasses. His expression of boredom remained unchanged. Body language strongly suggested he was resisting the urge to pace, and he obviously had no one to talk with while the crowd bustled around him.

Paralyzed with indecision, Dar failed to notice a pair of talkative police officers elbow their way through the patrons ahead of her. They went into the trading post without a word spoken to the man in denim. He seemed just as disinterested in them. Dar was still slowly summoning the courage she would need to brazenly walk past him when half a dozen customers walked out with their arms full of packages. They were followed by the pair of peace officers. They closed the thick, heavy door behind them.

"Sorry, folks!" one of them spoke loudly. "The store needs to be closed for one hour. Please come back later."

Disappointed murmurs echoed through the crowd. They dispersed without questions.

Dar stomped away from the man in denim, not sure if she should be angry or ashamed. Was he getting away from her or was she getting away from him? The vexing question was distracting while she walked—just enough to make her panic when she was approached by both of the cops she'd seen earlier.

"Good morning," one of them offered while the other looked over his shoulder. "I am Officer Hicks and my friend here is Officer Monroe."

"Good morning, sirs."

"Would you please come with us?" the officer asked.

Dar blushed. "What have I done?"

"You're not in trouble," Monroe informed her kindly without taking his eyes off the happenings around him.

Hicks smiled. "That's right, miss. The Taggerts are no friends of ours. We're just trying to keep the peace."

"They killed my parents!" she blurted uncontrollably.

"Not so loud," Hicks admonished severely.

"And my brother!" she added sharply.

"Hey!" the lookout barked at her. "Be smart. We're trying to help you!"

The leading officer came one step closer. "Please, let's get you to some place safer. Then, we'll see what sorts out."

Dar's outrage would not be quenched. She backed away. "They're going to kill me!"

Hicks pointed at his badge. "They won't make a move against you as long as they can see one of these. There are two of us, right?"

The other cop nodded. "Twice the protection. Bet on it."

"Where are we going?"

The assertive officer pointed at the guarded enclave gate. "Inside, behind those walls. All the good stuff and the best people are in there. Not even the Taggerts can touch you in there. Give us a chance, will you? We're here to help!"

The officers flanked Dar as they walked. "I recognized one of them," she explained while they approached the gate. "He was at our place nearly two days ago—"

"Slow down," Hicks entreated with casual tone that was forced. "Taggerts are like roaches. They show up all of a sudden, especially when you're not looking for them. Please, just be cool until we're inside the gate."

Dar began to notice the slow, measured way in which the officers walked, with their hands at their sides, their heads turning from left to right in an effort to see everything. They looked and sounded much calmer than she felt. She felt more self-conscious when they walked around the line of people who were waiting patiently to enter the enclave. She could feel curious gazes suspiciously questioning everything about her.

Hicks waved at the nearest guard wearing body armor. The muscular man gestured with a gloved hand.

"Get on through," Hicks urged. "Let's go. Trust me. If they didn't know where you are before, they do now."

Dar reminded herself that she wasn't in trouble, despite the fact that walking through the fortified gate made her feel guilty. Passing through a long mid-morning shadow cast by the earthworks surrounding the "good stuff" of Belmore, she tried not to dwell on the stories her grandparents had told of the need for such walls and how they were built using rocks, dirt, wreckage, and—when they ran out of construction equipment—manual labor.

Accepted wisdom suggested that dozens, hundreds, or even thousands of dead workers were hastily buried in any enclave's network of walls. Depending on the size of a place, that number could be unimaginable. As grim as that common knowledge was, it did tend to explain the sentiment of sacredness that people attributed to the enclave they lived in. For them, high earth walls represented their last, best hope in an uncertain world that was still traumatized by the past.

Officer Monroe broke in to her gruesome contemplation. "Give me your piece."

"Excuse me?"

Monroe pointed at a nearby sign. "No guns. What did you think I meant?"

"Never mind," Dar demurred defensively, handing over the pistol.

Monroe ejected the clip. "Did you know this thing isn't loaded?"

Dar blanched. "I, uh—you know."

The officer snickered. He handed the weapon to Hicks. "Yeah, sure."

Hicks put the clip back in to the semiautomatic pistol before wedging it into his belt. "Do you know how to use this?"

Dar nodded. "Of course I do. My parents wanted me and my brother to understand the difference between life and death. In the fall, they'd have us shoot some of the hogs and some of the cattle for slaughter. You know what? That's a really strange question to be asking me right now, in a place like this. What makes you think—?"

"Don't worry about it. Just had to be sure." he said, then changed the subject, "I grew up on a farm near Yelm. Ever been there?"

"No."

He gestured to a long, wide street. "Go that way. My parents yelled at me all the time to keep my guns unloaded until we had a need to use them. I think that's what kept me from killing both of my brothers and our kid sister. Did you and your brother get along?"

"Yes," she sniffled.

Hicks chimed in as they approached a busy intersection. "Looks like you might have a fan," he said without breaking stride. "As we cross the street, look slowly to your left."

Dar pivoted to see a tall man wearing a cowboy-style hat leaning against a lamppost. Hicks coughed. "Don't stare. That's Ben Taggert, usually smarter than one-eyed Sorel. Usually, but not always."

Ben watched her go with keen interest. She tried to memorize his face before he was out of her sight. She was speechless for several minutes while they walked.

"That way," Hicks directed. "See the big black and white car near the next intersection? Over there. That's where we're going."

Dar marveled at the spotless police cruiser when they got closer. "Does it run?"

"Yes, it does," Monroe said with some pride. "It's the only one we've got—and it goes like a bat out of Hell!"

Dar admired the clean car. She took a moment to walk around it. Faded stickers in the windows read: *U.S. Army Reserve*, *Washington National Guard*, and surprisingly; *Haven Site Access* followed by the numbers seven, six, eight, and five.

Her empty stomach rumbled just as her jaw dropped. "Do you happen to know if there is a Haven Site around here?"

Both of the officers laughed.

She looked up at the old, weathered, precinct building. "What is so funny? Is there anything—?"

Hicks raised a hand to stall her. "It's okay. You're going be fine. Are you hungry?"

"I can eat," she nodded enthusiastically.

He gestured. "Just down the street, there's a place where they do a first-rate hot dog. Come on inside and have a talk with our Captain and I'll bring you that hot dog myself."

Monroe opened a heavy door to a noisy lobby. "The Taggerts never come in here."

Dar shifted the load on her back. She looked up and down the street, silently envying the people who seemed to be doing whatever they wanted or needed to without fear of reprisal.

Acting on a need to have some control over her life, she smiled at the waiting cops. "Hot dogs first, then I'll talk."

CHAPTER SEVEN

Captain Drake returned from his self-appointed rounds of Belmore just after 11 a.m. He was met by the enclave's senior detective in a narrow, dim hallway near his office.

"Sorel and five riders galloped out of here about thirty minutes ago," the man told him. "The merchies I talked to said they bought oats for their horses. That says fast movement to me. Nothing strange about the normal run of supplies they picked up."

"Did they stock up on bullets?" Drake asked.

Cullins shook his bald head. "No. Can't hardly blame them. If they are after the girl, they won't be expecting much of a fight."

The veteran officer took off his peaked cap. "Ben is still around here, somewhere. He stuck to me like glue for the first half of my patrol."

The plain-clothed officer grimaced. "Must've expected the girl to file a complaint."

"Yeah, well," Drake exhaled, "that's not going to happen. Where is she?"

"Waiting in your office with Hicks," the man clarified. "Bellamy went for hot dogs."

Drake looked up and down the empty hallway. "D'you think Bellamy is ready for field work?"

Cullins was optimistic. "Four years on patrol, two more as my shadow. Yes."

Drake leaned closer. "Ben Taggert likes to run his mouth."

"Tell me something I don't know!"

The senior officer scowled. "He seems quite convinced the girl is going to Delphi."

"School," Cullins deduced.

"How is she doing?"

Cullins chuckled. "Not happy about being picked up. She thinks we ambushed her."

Drake shrugged it off. "Right then. Feed her, put her someplace safe overnight, and she's out of here tomorrow when the train moves. Put Bellamy in cruddy clothes. Send her with what's-her-name as an insurance policy, just to be sure the Taggerts don't spill blood in our jurisdiction."

Cullins liked what he heard. "Give me about half an hour or so to put this together. You know, we could get Delphi to owe us one if we tip them off. Bellamy hands off to their badges immediately after the train arrives. As much as they like to pretend they're law and order, most of the Taggerts won't interfere with real cops. That lets the girl get off to school. Good guys win."

"This time."

* * *

Drake met with Dar in his office. Sitting behind his desk, he laid his peaked cap on a stack of papers that would have to be read later.

"You've been through a lot. I don't see any point in sugar-coating this. I want— I ask— Please, keep your fight out of my town."

Dar sat on a creaky wooden chair with her father's rucksack on the floor next to her. Events of the last two days were just as eye-opening to her as they had been traumatic. "How can you—"

Officer Hicks leaned forward in his chair. "Come on, think about this for a minute. We're not standing around. We do what we can, when we can. The rest is compromise. Tumwater is at least twenty times bigger than we are, maybe more. The Taggerts have more hired guns than you would believe."

"He's right," Drake stated succinctly.

Dar was too tired to be angry. "Do you know what they're doing out there?"

The older man folded his hands. "Yes. I know what they've done. I know what they're still doing. I can even tell you why."

"They're not the law—"

"They think they are," Drake exclaimed irately.

"*Why*?" Dar wanted to know.

The captain sat back, his chair squeaked. He gestured at a row of dusty telephones perched on a shelf. "The Collapse was more than a downfall of governments or the death of nations. It was a long, slow, technological backslide. For as long as they could, local, state, and national governments coordinated with each other. They shared resources until there was nothing left to pass around."

"I know all that," Dar protested mildly.

Drake took off his badge and laid it on the desk. "Food and medicine were all gone weeks before those phones stopped ringing. All they had left to go on was bureaucracy. Lots of laws and a million rules that justified the authority elected leaders needed to keep what was left of the peace. Laws don't feed hungry people, so they forgot about them."

Hicks coughed sarcastically. "Taggerts have been rigging the elections in Tumwater for more than a century. Each new mayor is always a Taggert. They go out of their way to remind people around them about all the emergency regulations that were in effect when, like the captain says, those phones went quiet."

"That is so wrong!"

Drake sighed his exasperation. "It is. When we're not busy telling stories about hostile tech and bloodthirsty machines, we lie to each other about

Haven and what it was or might still be. That mythology is a drug that makes us feel better, but it blinds us to the Taggerts of the world."

Dar was feeling combative. She wanted to ask about the Haven sticker she'd seen on the police car. This didn't seem like the time or place to indulge that impulse. "What are you going to do about it—them!"

Hicks remained silent.

Drake shook his head. "Right now, we do the best we can. Our gates are open to strangers like yourself. We may not be able to stop the Taggerts, but we can slow them down. Doesn't seem like much. It might even be just enough to give you a head start. All I'm asking for is a little bit of understanding. Keep your fight out of my town and you'll always be welcome here."

Dar was incredulous. "I'm supposed to be on my way while these guys get away with murder?"

"That's about the size of it," Drake conceded pessimistically. "We'll put you on the train to Delphi. One of our officers will be with you all the way. The Taggerts' influence doesn't extend to Delphi. Not yet, anyway. I've been told the school you're going to has a dozen teachers and a hundred students. That's enough witnesses to ensure your safety for a long time. Someday, if we're still here, we'd like to have you back. You'd make a good addition to the community."

Hicks moved in his chair. "Go ahead," he encouraged her. "Tell him about Marsh."

"You know him?" Drake guessed.

Dar nodded. She put a hand to her face. "He's been showing his wares to us for as long as I can remember. We just bought some new glasses from him for my birthday."

"What does he say about us?"

She shrugged. "He mentions Belmore from time to time. I kind of get the impression he has a shop here."

"Should we trust him?" Hicks asked his boss.

Drake looked carefully at his wristwatch before focusing his attention on Dar. "You need a place to stay overnight. I need you to be somewhere Ben Taggert won't think to look for you. Most people are not in the habit of overnighting with the kind of person Marsh is. Has he ever given you any reason to not trust him?"

Hicks nudged her. "Has he ever tried to get friendly?"

"No!"

"Do you trust him?" Drake demanded. "He's been known to sell a few things we didn't approve of. Scavengers lucky enough to survive the ruins like to trade with him. That, by itself, isn't really enough for me to lock him up. Wish I could. Really, I do."

Dar snorted. "He's not a pervert, if that's what you're asking. We let him sleep on the couch sometimes. Never any trouble, not like you mean. Mom was careful about what we fed him—no beans! He could have really bad gas."

Drake looked at Hicks. "Go. Find Marsh and run this by him. Then, get back to me."

"He'll expect to be paid," Hicks anticipated.

Drake picked up his badge and put it on. "Remind him that it's a good idea to have some of our good will, especially when he gets caught with contraband inside the walls."

"You make it sound like that happens a lot," Dar supposed.

Drake pushed his chair back. "Not your problem," he admonished while standing up.

"Please give Officer Hicks your full cooperation. The next 24 hours are going to be a little crazy. For now, I need you to let us make the arrangements. If Marsh doesn't pan out, we'll find somebody else for you to overnight with. Don't worry about the train or the price of a ticket. It'll be my—our—pleasure to get you on your way without any interference from the Taggerts. Makes me feel good already, just knowing how much Ben and Sorel are going to get yelled at for their failure to put you in the ground."

Hicks got to his feet. "C'mon, let's go. I'll introduce you to—"

"Can I have my gun?"

Drake looked at his subordinate.

Hicks reassured him. "Her weapon and ammunition are impounded. I wrote out the receipt myself. She was searched by Bellamy when we brought her in—the full pat-down. No drugs."

Dar stood up suddenly. "Hey!"

Drake looked apologetic. "A pretty face and a hard luck story are always good camouflage. Sometimes people use them to get away with very bad things. You know what I mean. We do appreciate your honesty. It makes our job easier. I'm sorry that you have to be put through any of this. Hicks, sign over Miss Lambert's property to Officer Bellamy. She can give all of it back to her when they're safely on the train."

* * *

Marsh was completely thunderstruck when the inquisitive Officer Hicks unexpectedly appeared in the open delivery doorway of his warehouse. "I'm sorry, would you please say that again?"

Hicks took off his hat before coming inside. "Please, excuse the interruption. I know it's just on high noon. You must be ready for lunch. I'm here about Darlene Lambert."

"Y-yes," the merchant stammered, "Yes, of course! What can I do for you?"

Hicks looked left and right while he spoke. "How well do you know the family?"

Marsh noticed the officer's intense perusal of the interior. "Quite well, actually. They are good customers. Known the children most of their lives. Why do you ask?"

The experience cop took a step closer. "When was the last time you saw them?"

"Two days ago," Marsh recounted conservatively. "Weather permitting, I'm out there once a month. To answer your next question, I sold them a pair of glasses for their daughter."

"Notice anything strange while you were in that area?"

"No," the merchant replied casually. "It's farmland. They go to work when the sun comes up; they go to bed when the sun goes down. Strange is not in their vocabulary. All they seem to want are engine parts for anything that still runs or the little things that make life easier, like glasses."

The officer continued to scrutinize Marsh. He tucked his hat under one arm. "You make it sound good. Almost makes me want to live out there."

The entrepreneur's expression soured. "The rustic life is not for me. I'm getting too old for it. What's all this about Darlene Lambert? Has something happened?"

"You might say that," Hicks indicated slowly while trying to make up his mind about Marsh. "Her parents and brother were killed."

"Is she all right?" Marsh asked empathetically.

"She's a survivor," the officer nodded. "How do you feel about the Taggerts?"

Marsh knew he should be hesitant or afraid. He licked his lips in an attempt to appear uneasy. "I don't do anything for them voluntarily. They scare me. That's why I'm here, in Belmore."

Hicks began to pace. Marsh's opinion of the Taggerts was nothing more than he expected. "You've got a place like this in Tumwater, don't you?"

"Yes," Marsh confessed benignly. "Bigger, actually. Three employees, if you can call them that. They're stealing from me now, I just know it."

The office paused to glance down a long row of shelves filled with boxes and crates. "I couldn't manage a place like this by myself. I'd need help. How many employees do you have here?"

Marsh knew when he was being interrogated. Suppression his inward indignation, he slouched in an effort to convey outward deference. "I'm sure Detective Cullins has told you all about me. I give temporary work to the scavengers who come through when they want to stay for a while. Some do, just to rest. Then, they're on their way to search for the next bonanza."

Hicks turned to look down another aisle. "Do you miss it?"

Marsh recoiled. "Scavenging? No, not even a little! Don't get me wrong," he backtracked, "I've got my share of wild stories to tell for the price of a beer, but no, I don't miss it."

Hicks gestured at a dark corner of the warehouse. "Do you mind if I look around?"

"I don't think that will be necessary," Marsh objected.

The officer appeared to relax. "How well do you know Darlene Lambert?"

"She's a good kid," Marsh declared simply. "Can I assume from what you're not saying that the Taggerts had something to do with her situation?"

"What if it does?"

Marsh knew he shouldn't hesitate. "How can I help?"

The officer's mood brightened. "I'm glad you asked. We'd be grateful if you could loan her a place to sleep, just for the night. I'm sure you've got a private place in here somewhere. Something with a door that locks? We'd make arrangement for dinner—"

"I'd be glad to help!" the merchant agreed before the officer was able to verbalize more conditions. "No matter how temporary they are, I always make a point of providing rooms for my employees. It makes up for what I don't pay them."

"Show me," Hicks insisted.

"This way!" Marsh directed with a wave. "Feeding her won't be a problem," he assured while they made their way through a maze of shelves to a trio of improvised bedrooms with scarred wooden doors. "As you can see for yourself, we have beds with mattresses and adequate lighting for the usual things."

Hicks walked through each room quickly. "We'll have an extra badge walking through this neighborhood tonight."

"If you say so," Marsh acknowledged.

"What am I smelling?"

Marsh pointed down a dark passageway. "Two bathrooms and showers are that way. End of the hall is my kitchen. You're smelling my own recipe, refined over many years. I always keep a pot of beans warming on the stove, ready to eat!"

The officer looked into the dimly lit kitchen, at the large simmering pot on a stove. "Do you have anything else to eat?"

"Why would I?"

Hicks was diplomatically silent. He followed Marsh back through the warehouse, to the loading area and the front door. "We appreciate the help. Officer Monroe will bring Dar back over here before sunset."

"Of course."

Hicks put his hat on. “You remember Detective Bellamy?”

“Yes, I do.”

The officer stepped out in to daylight, looking up and down the street. “She’ll come by first thing in the morning to get her. Now that you have some idea of what Dar has been through, I hope you won’t upset her with a lot of questions.”

“Never!”

Hicks looked at his watch. “If all goes well, she should be on her way before you have beans for breakfast.”

CHAPTER EIGHT

A clock on the wall of Marsh's sparse, humid kitchen told Dar it was just after 7 p.m. Sitting on one side of a wobbly wooden table across from her host, she tried not to think about the plastic chair that was hurting her bottom or to stare disconsolately at the bowl of beans in front of her.

"You know," he growled sympathetically with his mouth full, "might seem strange, but I can relate. I was about your age—maybe a little younger—when my parents lost everything. We were attacked. That's what got me in to scavenging. We really didn't have any other good choices."

Dar couldn't help thinking about the random assortment of food inside her rucksack. Every last crumb of it now seemed much more desirable than what she was trying to eat.

Marsh pointed his spoon at her. "Trust me, I know how you feel. All that farm food you're used is high cuisine when compared to this. Beans are cheap and they mix with almost anything."

Dar used her own spoon to take a bite and swallow. "Carrots, potatoes, and beans."

"Yes!" Marsh praised through another mouthful, "You have good taste. Sorry if this is insulting. You might as well dig in while it's warm. Beans are never as good when they get cold.

His encouragement didn't help. Dar ate silently until the bowl was empty. Hours of unending boredom had slowly worn her down long before she'd been escorted to Marsh's home away from home.

"You'd like Tumwater," he said absentmindedly while taking away the used dishes. "Once you get past the Taggerts, it's a nice place."

"Why are you here?" she asked just to be polite.

It was the kind of opening he was looking for. Marsh let the bowls and spoons clatter into a nearby sink. "So. Let me ask you a question. Have you ever wanted to be alone? Not permanently, just to have some time to yourself. A few days or a couple of weeks? Does that mean anything to you?"

Dar found herself nodding. She brushed food crumbs off her shirt and vest. "I have."

He leaned casually against the sink. "I never really did know what that meant until I left home. Crawling through the ruins of places you've never heard of with people I can't remember was a rush. All that danger and adrenaline was like living twice normal speed. Then, all of a sudden, I'm here and I have time to think."

Dar was mesmerized by the confession. It was enough to allow her to ignore some of her own grief. "The Taggerts don't give you a lot of time to think. Is that it?"

Marsh made himself take a breath. Prying for information was second-nature to him. Dar's youthful idealism and inexperience made her an easier target than some adults, though even she would eventually figure out what he was doing. "No. Not really. The Taggerts aren't hard to figure out. They just want you to do things their way. Some of what they want isn't all bad, either. Law and order is good for business. It allows me to sleep safe. Problem is, I get more of a say in what I do when I'm here."

Dar shifted in her uncomfortable chair. "The cops told me—"

"Please!" Marsh exploded, "Those are the same guys who want you out of their hair! They say a lot of things about me, some of which are true, but— but— I don't sell anything that would harm the good people of this community!"

"I believe you!" she relented. "Can we sit somewhere else? This chair is no fun."

Marsh stepped away from the sink. "You want fun?"

Dar got to her feet unsteadily. "Right about now, I'd settle for anything that isn't beans. No offense."

Marsh faked indifference. "None taken. Come on, let me show you something fun."

Dar's dread became curiosity. She followed him deep into the warehouse.

The older man paused to flip a series of old-fashioned light switches. Both of them blinked when bright overhead lamps came on.

He pointed with pride. "This entire aisle, all the way to the end, it's everything in the world that matters to me."

His grand gesture had the intended effect; Dar was dazzled. Rusty metal shelves were piled from floor to ceiling with a dizzying assortment of recognizable items, objects, and things—much more than she could easily identify at a glance.

"Amazing," she said enviously while shuffling slowly past more loot than she'd ever seen. "I couldn't imagine having this much stuff."

Marsh kept his distance. "You have been through a lot," he empathized carefully. "Officer Monroe filled me in. I am sorry for your loss. There's no way I can imagine what it's like."

"You said your parents were attacked?"

"We were," he recalled as the neared the end of the aisle. "I did my part to get them back on their feet. Then, I went my own way."

Dar turned to face him. "You never went back?"

"No," Marsh admitted. "Well, that's not true. I went back for funerals. My father, then my mother. They were both gone by the time I was thirty. I never did get educated. Not like the kind of schooling you got, or the one you're going to."

Dar shrugged. "Can't go back," she lamented. "Taggerts took the farm. All I seem to have left is school. Do you really think—?"

Marsh worked fast to interrupt her melancholy. She'd stop talking if she was too sad. "Are you kidding?" he blustered. "Half the people in this enclave would gladly sell their last blanket for the kind of life you had! My own parents didn't have much to give me, but they made all this possible. They worked hard, saved what they could, and that gave me a good example. What's the word I'm looking for?"

"Role model," Dar offered.

"Yeah," he agreed fluidly. "Your parents, and that knucklehead brother of yours, they are your role models. Remember who they were and try to be like that. Whatever it was. You know what I mean."

Dar did understand. She moved closer to a pile of school books on a nearby shelf. "Have you read these?"

"I have," Marsh confirmed. "I've sold at least a dozen copies of those books to Helen. I know she put them to good use."

"Any idea what kind of books they have for high school?"

Marsh was enthusiastic. "Over here," he moved to show her. "Here. On the end."

Dar went to the shelf space he indicated. She picked up a large, heavy textbook that was remarkably clean. "Algebra Basics," she read from the cover. "That's math, right?"

"Yes," Marsh affirmed. "Everything you see there in the pile was fabricated just a few years ago. I saw the machine that did it, too."

Dar bent over to slowly read more titles. "Advanced math, chemistry, computer use. Do they really teach all of that in high school?"

"You're the one who's going. You'll have to tell me after you've been there."

She laughed. "You never went?"

He conspicuously brushed at his pot belly. "Do I look like I went to high school?

"You seem rich enough," Dar appraised with a sweeping gesture. "Why not go now?"

Marsh pretended to think about that proposition. Dar wasn't opening up to him as much as he'd hoped she would. Time to change tactics.

"Wealth does not buy experience," he told her as plainly as he could. "Knowing what I know right now, there's a lot I would do differently. Everything in this warehouse is here because I did something right and something wrong. That includes my not-so-humble self, me. Ah, before you ask, yes. I would trade a lot of this for a different set of dreams."

Dar snickered. "Hard to imagine you having pie-in-the-sky dreams."

"What if I did?" he responded indignantly. "I was young once, a long time ago. I had a few wild and crazy ideas. There might even still be one or two of them floating around inside my head. Wouldn't that be a shock?"

"Like what?" she challenged lightheartedly, "Name one thing you still dream about."

Marsh pretended to be reluctant. "Well, okay. There is one thing I'm pretty sure you can relate to. Come with me. Laugh or joke just once at what I'm about to show you, and I'll throw you out on your ear!"

"I wouldn't—"

Marsh was bellicose. He pointed at a nearby darkened room. "I'll do it!" he bellowed. "I don't care if you are walking out of here in the morning. Nobody makes fun of me!"

Dar was plaintive while she followed the irate man. "I won't! Besides, I'm going on the train. It's the fastest way to Delphi; hopefully, it's quick enough to keep me one step ahead of the Taggerts."

Marsh muttered as if he was still offended. "For your sake, I hope so. It's one thing to get ripped off by the Taggerts. That I can live with. There will always be more loot! I can't imagine what it would be like if they wanted me six feet under. Being dead is not something you can buy your way out of or back from."

Dar followed him into the small room, expecting to see the kind of thing adults often fondly reminisced about when they shared favorite memories—candy, junk food, and toys. She gasped when he turned on the bright overhead light.

The room was a lot smaller than she had expected it to be. Hundreds of individual items adorned the walls. Most of them were magazine covers, newspaper clippings, and ragged pages torn from every imaginable form of publication. All of them related in some way to Haven Sites located in what had been Washington State.

Marsh stood aside. He waited patiently for the sight of it all to have the desired effect. For as long as he could remember, Dar hadn't been able to pass up a chance to harmlessly speculate about the subject of Haven—what it had been or might still be. In his estimation, she was largely unaware that a countless number of adults had already spent the best years of their short, danger-filled lives in passionate pursuit of something they could never seem to find.

He was aware of the power to enthrall that Haven mythology could have over anyone, including himself.

As a young man hoping to make his family rich, he had set off on his own five-year odyssey. In the company of good friends that he later outlived, they starved and nearly froze to death before any shots were fired. Returning home to bury his father, then his mother, Marsh gave up the dream—until he had found what was on the walls of the room that Dar now stood in.

"Wow," she breathed.

"Most of what you see is useless," Marsh declared spitefully. "The rest of it is enough to keep me awake at night. Only half of this was tacked up when I first found the place. The other half of this mess is just what I've collected over the years. Never have been able to organize it to make sense."

"It's amazing," Dar marveled.

Marsh savored the moment. "Yes, it is."

"What does it mean?"

He laughed. "Solve that riddle and we'll both be rich. I'll even cut you in for half."

She stared at him skeptically.

Marsh coughed. "I'm serious," he told her calmly. "You're looking at the bits and pieces that drive people crazy. They spend everything they have for supplies, and the next time you see them, they're babbling nonsense or they're dead."

Dar took off her glasses. She stepped closer to read some of what was on the wall. "Governor declares Seattle a hostile technology zone; many residents are forced to flee. Here's document that looks like the text of a law, something about national emergency. This newspaper clipping says; Congress votes funding for large-scale resettlement plan. Here, here, and here," she pointed at different articles, "they all say something about Haven sites. S-i-t-e-s, that's plural. Means more than one. How many could there be?"

Marsh was about to guess when a powered bell on the far side of the warehouse rang.

"Who visits you at this time of night?"

The merchant smiled. "That would be a customer or a delivery. Either way, I—"

Dar rubbed her backside. "I really don't want to sit for a while. Can I just stay here? I've never seen a collection like this before."

"Say no more!" he consented with a flourish. "Please, just do me the favor of staying out of sight. Some of my customers are—how can I say this kindly?—rather eccentric. They don't like to do business when there is an audience."

Dar began to think Marsh really was a criminal. "That's okay," she told him blandly. "The cops already gave me a long speech. I'm supposed to stay out of sight until they put me on the train."

The bell rang a second time. Marsh turned to go. "Yeah. I never have liked riding trains by myself. So many strange faces, always looking at me without saying a word."

"I won't be alone," Dar said while putting on her glasses. "Go ahead. I won't get in your way. They'll never even know I'm here. If you're still busy when I'm done, I'll just go to bed."

Within seconds of the merchant's departure, Dar was deeply immersed in the sea of clues scattered all over the walls around her. They explained a lot about the scope and scale of what Haven had been. That context was enlightening. Insight allowed her to understand how any one person who didn't know any better might come to the conclusion that Haven was just one place. "Haven really was more than one sanctuary," she realized out loud.

Her heart skipped a beat when she got close enough to make out what was printed on a strangely familiar sheet of old paper that was yellowed with age. Something about its curling edges and the way it had once been folded convinced her she had seen it before.

Feeling it with both hands, she stepped back just enough to clearly read from the page.

"Page one of two," she made out. "Where have I seen that?"

Acting on a hunch, she went back to the room where her rucksack lay on a lumpy bed. Turning on a weak light, she hurriedly unzipped the pack. Peeling it open, she rummaged for the fistful of old papers that she'd rifled through the previous day. Finding them only made her more frantic when she realized that one of the folded pages was missing!

Dar looked over her shoulder at the open door and the dark hallway. She must've dropped the page when she fled so hastily from the side of the road. Somebody had found it. How had Marsh gotten his hands on it?

Dar sat on the edge of the bed. "Somebody knows more than they're telling."

* * *

Marsh got a surprise of his own when he looked through a peephole in the side door. Through the tiny aperture, he saw Frank in his distinctive denim, grumpily loitering in the cool night air. He opened the door. "Are you out of your mind? Darlene is still here!"

"Don't blame this on me!" the henchman complained. "Ben was impatient. Tell me something and I'm outta here!"

Marsh was mad. "They're going to put her on the train to Delphi. Makes me think Drake is trying to avoid trouble."

"Are you sure?" Frank pressed. "Trust me, the Taggerts really don't like these guys."

"The feeling is mutual," Marsh replied sarcastically.

"Anything else?" Frank prodded.

The bullied merchant stalled by looking over his shoulder, first left and then right. Just enough time to think about his risky relationship with the Taggerts and how the next words he spoke might somehow endanger Dar. That hesitation was the closest thing to guilt he was capable of feeling. "She was just starting to open up to me, when you rang! If there is anything else, I'll tell it to Ben—*in the morning*!"

Marsh slammed the door shut. Dar didn't actually say she would be travelling with an escort. She might've been referring to all the other people on the train when she said she wouldn't be alone. Turning his back on the locked door, the aggravated entrepreneur decided he would console himself with the minor omission. That way, he'd have no hand in whatever the Taggerts did to the target of their hostility.

* * *

Dar summoned her willpower. She'd been clamping down on her suspicions before Marsh reappeared in the small shrine to Haven.

He approached noisily, before shuffling into the harshly lit room. "What a waste of time!" he complained with a rude gesture.

"What did they want?" she asked with her back turned.

"Nothing that matters," he grumbled. "Just because people bring me things doesn't mean I know where everything is!"

Dar resettled her glasses without turning to look at him. She casually approached the creased page on the wall, caressing it with a finger thoughtfully. "This looks interesting. Where did you get it?"

Marsh inwardly cursed himself for being so careless. Knowing that some truth might save him some grief, he inhaled before getting closer. "Yes.

That's new. I traded for it yesterday. Just between you and me, I probably got robbed! Oh, well. It seemed like a good investment at the time. Haven't really had a spare minute to give it a closer look. What do you think?"

She pretended to study the document. "Who did you get this from?"

"Some guy," the merchant rambled vaguely. "People in my line of work don't always like to use names. They prefer to let what they're hustling do all the talking. In this case, what you see is what you get."

Dar nodded without speaking.

For as long as she could remember, Marsh had been proud of the deals he made. Even when he got ripped off, he showed some kind of respect for anyone who could fleece him. Knowing how much he enjoyed bragging about profit or complaining about loss, the insensitive tone of his voice was almost audible. He was lying.

"Didn't cost much?"

He responded reflexively. "No, not really."

She turned to face him. "That's too bad. Something like that has to be worth something to somebody."

Marsh knew his reluctant guest was being provocative, proving to him that she was angry about the artifact he had foolishly pinned up on the wall. A part of him regretted the decision only because he didn't wish her any further harm. She'd suffered enough. The rest of him was offended by her insolence.

"Just out of curiosity, what do you make of it? I'm no expert, but it seems to me —well, you could get the idea from those words that there is or was a Haven Site around here, somewhere."

Despite her anger, his theory was hard to resist. "I can see how you might think that."

Dar was angry with herself. She was to blame for losing the document. As deceptive and annoying as he was being, Marsh was not at fault for trading with one of the Taggerts to get it. As much as she dearly wanted to reclaim it, she also felt a need to be cautious. The explicit verbal warnings given to her by Captain Drake, Officer Hicks, and Officer Monroe couldn't be ignored.

Marsh saw from her body language that Dar had clammed up. "Don't worry about it. I'm just guessing! Years before I decided to live here, there was a rumor about some guy who traded a lot of good loot for the most ordinary things—food, camping supplies, and the like. They say he lived outside the walls, somewhere deep in the forest. That was back when things were bad."

Dar was noncommittal. "My grandparents said something about it."

Marsh knew he needed to retreat. "Ask anyone who has lived here their whole life, they'll tell you the same story. Said he always came from the west and went back there, every time. You might be surprised how many people want to knock on my door, after they've heard that legend. It's always been profitable to equip them, so I stay."

Dar made up her mind. "Interesting story," she acknowledged with restraint. "That's the forest between here and Delphi?"

"That would be it," he confirmed. "There were some old roads through it. They got to be impassible after so many decades of neglect. Some of them were cleared when the rail line was put through to Delphi. You want some more beans?"

"No," she dissented. "I'm going to bed."

Marsh watched her leave the room before he turned off the light. She was gone from sight before he made his way back to the kitchen just after 9 p.m.

CHAPTER NINE

Dar couldn't sleep. Alone in the small sparse improvised bedroom, behind a locked door, she kept the light on. Conflicting emotions and the lumpy mattress wouldn't let her rest. The thought of undressing made her skin crawl. She kicked her shoes off and put them next to the bed. She carefully put her glasses on a small, dusty nightstand next to a lamp that didn't work. Her shoulders throbbed when she removed her multi-pocket vest. She tried to sleep with it hugged close.

As she dozed, spectral images from the last two days occupied her anxious mind. None of the memories were intense enough to be nightmares. All of them were disturbing in a way that was unreal and short-lived. A sudden series of remembered gunshots and brief glimpses of violence in the living room of her family home jolted her wide awake.

"I'm coming!" she heard herself shout.

She blinked forcefully. The bed rocked back and forth with the motion of her struggle. Her dingy surroundings were close enough to be seen clearly. The reality of her situation was too much. She sobbed uncontrollably into a stained pillow.

"I don't know what to do…"

In the distance, a trio of air horns howled. It was enough to make her sit up. "The train!" she reminded herself through a sniffle.

Sounds of strident snoring began to reach her through the door of the room she was in, coming from somewhere down the hall. Her wristwatch displayed 4 a.m. when she looked at it. She put both hands to her puffy face, releasing a long yawn. "Can't give up now," she told herself humorlessly. "Don't quit, don't quit, just don't do it!"

Marsh continued to snore while she used the bathroom and shower. The hot water was invigorating. Putting her stinky clothes back on was an unfriendly reminder of her unfortunate situation. Wiping the fog of steam off a mirror, she forced her hair into a shape that looked like she had tried to comb it.

The sonorous nasal vibration of the merchant's relentless snoring was suddenly accentuated by a long, loud fart.

Fatigue and the silliness of the moment were overpowering. She laughed at the mirror. "You are so messed up!" she ridiculed her reflection, "Jack would never let you forget about this if he was here to see it."

The mockery was sobering. Feeling through the pockets of her vest, she found her brush. Grooming her hair slowly, she focused on the bloodshot eyes staring back at her. "Stick to the plan. Get on the train and go to school. Finish school and make something of yourself. See what the Taggert problem looks like when you're not so damned scared, and maybe—just maybe—do something about it!"

Dar went through her things before zipping the rucksack closed. She put her hands in every pocket of her clothing and vest, then gave one quick touch to be sure her glasses were on.

Marsh was still snoring loudly when she turned off the light and left the room. Still feeling betrayed, she shouldered her backpack. Using her flashlight to make her way through the dark warehouse, she located the room full of assorted Haven keepsakes. She snatched the folded document off the wall.

"Page one of two!" she celebrated with a vengeful whisper.

The thrill of vindication made her overconfident. Seconds later, she was lost among the aisles and shelves of the innermost warehouse. Minutes of disoriented backtracking were humbling before she found a lane that brought her close enough to see an exit. Unlocking the door, she slipped out into the damp morning air.

* * *

The long slow walk away from Marsh's warehouse toward the gate she knew about was discouraging. Streetlights, traffic signs, and the absence of trash in the road or on the sidewalks made her feel out of place. Stopping at an intersection to get her bearings, she was approached by a lone police officer wearing rain gear.

"You look like you're lost," he said by way of a greeting.

"Tell me about it," she complained. "I'm going to the west gate. Can you point me in the right direction?"

He gestured with a long-handled flashlight. "That way, four blocks. Where are you going at this hour?"

"Just going to wait for the train."

The officer pulled up the sleeve of his raincoat to have a fast look at his digital watch. "It's just on 5:30. It'll be daylight in an hour or so. You're not from around here?"

"No, sir. Just passing through."

The attentive man looked her up and down. "You've got your pick of places to eat. A lot of them are opening right about now. Today, the train is going to Delphi. Is that where you want to go?"

"It is," she admitted apathetically.

"You don't sound so sure about that," he observed.

Dar glanced up and down the dew-drenched street. Pedestrians and shopkeepers were starting to appear. "Thanks. A lot of things have changed for me in the last few days."

"How are you holding up?" he asked.

She thought about the reflection of herself she had seen in Marsh's bathroom mirror. "I'm getting it figured out," she determined with a self-deprecating shrug. "Sometimes, things happen to people when they shouldn't. It's not my fault when they do. I just need to know what I want and how to get it without hurting myself or anyone else."

"Good idea," he agreed. "The train is that way. Get yourself something warm to eat. Lines form at 7. They start loading at half past. Most of the time, they're on their way by 8. I wish you well!"

* * *

Dar found a long bench on the elevated train platform just before 6 a.m. She put her rucksack down before sitting on what turned out to be wet wood.

"That is just great!"

Ill-tempered in the predawn twilight, she swore when the condensed moisture soaked her pants. Draining as the lack of sleep was, she felt more comfortable out in the open, where she could see other people and they could see her. Refusing to move, Dar opened her rucksack, grabbed a candy bar, and unwrapped it. She nibbled, silently defying the dampness that was enveloping her. Sunrise was obscured by low-hanging clouds threatening rain.

Time passed slowly. Dar watched as foot traffic approaching the west gate picked up. Men and women of all ages stood in line with the same casual attitudes she'd experienced a day earlier. A few of them appeared to be in her age range, causing Dar to wonder about their interests and motivations. What did they like? What were they afraid of? How many of them would she eventually see in school, at Delphi?

Her watch read 7:15 a.m. when the lines at the west gate began to diminish. Air horns in the distance announced the approach of the rumbling train. Passengers and their baggage began to gather on the platform. Light mist fell. Railroad employees started selling tickets. Dar stood and shouldered her pack. She was still looking for an opening in the crowd when a female voice called out to her.

Dar immediately recognized Detective Bellamy when she saw her. "Hello!"

"Hello yourself!" Bellamy approached wearing a vest, stocking hat, clothes, boots, and a backpack that was similar to Dar's. "You're a hard person to find."

"I had to get out of there!" Dar confessed.

In her late twenties, Bellamy was slightly taller than Dar. She elbowed her way through the crowd to stand nearby. "I don't blame you. Marsh is a lot to put up with. Did he say or do anything I should know about?"

Dar scowled. "Nothing like that. I guess he was always a different person when he came out to our farm. We were just paying customers to him, not real friends. Too bad. I used to like him. He's probably mad at me."

Bellamy adjusted the pack on her back. "He wasn't happy to see me, that's for sure! From what I could see just walking through his place, you did leave a pile of wet towels on the bathroom floor."

"Yeah," Dar laughed.

The detective looked at her seriously. "I'm sure it's funny. Was there anything else you may have done that might not be so humorous to him?"

"I dunno."

Bellamy relented. "Okay, then. Before we go get our tickets, there are a few things I need you to understand. From now on, just call me Bellamy. Don't say anything about cops. Pretend I'm your big sister. That's why I dressed like you, so I can blend in. I'm your disguise and you are mine."

Dar did get it. "Two people travelling together. What about my pistol?"

Bellamy pointed at the far side of the platform. "Tickets, then food—in that order! When I'm not starving and we're on the train away from here, we talk about your gun."

"What about the Taggerts?"

Bellamy looked around. "What about them?"

"What if one of them gets on the train?" Dar worried.

The officer turned again. "You're not the first person to get their special treatment. You probably won't be the last. Trust me. We're good at making travel arrangements. Just put the whole thing out of your mind. That includes Marsh; he's not your problem."

* * *

Ben Taggert was angry. Standing in the open delivery door of Marsh's warehouse, he grabbed the stuttering, apologetic merchant by the collar of his wrinkled shirt. "You are getting to be a real problem, do you know that?"

Marsh had a lot of practice with talking himself out of a beating. "It's not my fault! For all I know, she saw Frank or heard his voice! I asked you to give me a free hand—"

Ben bowed his head and released his grip. "Yes. Yes, damn it—and I did agree!"

He turned, glaring suspiciously at the group of armed men waiting for his orders.

Marsh was shorter, though much heavier. As spineless as he could be, he'd never given any member of the Taggert family a good reason to hate him. If anything, his penchant for self-preservation was predictable enough to make him reliable.

Ben suppressed his hereditary temper, going so far as to smile before he reached out to smooth Marsh's shirt collar. "Yeah. Okay, then. Looks like we have a train to catch."

Marsh licked his lips. Of all the questionable things he'd ever done, this form of betrayal was always the hardest to live with. In the heat of the moment, he flirted with the idea that, just this once, a beating might not be so bad—especially if it prevented such an innocent person from being killed.

"Let's not be so hasty about this. She might be travelling with a cop. You know how Captain Drake is. He likes to put some things out of your reach. Come on inside and have some beans, let's talk. I'm sure we—"

"Frank!" Ben bellowed.

Frank separated himself from the group with two quick steps. "Yes, boss!"

Ben stepped away from Marsh. "I'm getting on that train!" he asserted vehemently. "Get your sorry butt over there. Have ten tickets for me when I get there. The rest of you, load your gear into packs. Use duffel bags if you have to. Pass the word to anyone who isn't here! All you, be on time for the train. Get yourself there in 15 minutes or less! I'll shoot anyone who finds a way to get left behind. Go. Go!"

* * *

Dar and Bellamy stood in an alley between two food vendors that was too narrow for most people to squeeze through. She ate a greasy hot dog with one hand while she fondled a big brass token in the other. "I give this to somebody when we get on?"

"Yes," Bellamy confirmed while eating her own hot dog. "Just put it in the bucket. This your first time on a train?"

Dar nodded while she ate. "Sometimes, we can hear it. The horns. Tracks are too far away from the farm to ever see it. I have wondered what it would be like to ride a train. Seems to be a lot of demand for it."

Bellamy licked her fingers and wiped them on her pants. "They mostly move people. Fruits, vegetables, and livestock are seasonal."

"I know," Dar acknowledged while she finished the last of her improvised breakfast. "We didn't always have enough extra to sell. When we did, my folks would bring it to Belmore. The last few harvests have been a little lean. I haven't been here in two years."

Bellamy looked at her watch. "Okay, they've already started boarding. Time to get serious. I'll give you your gun, but there are a few rules. First, don't ever travel with an unloaded weapon. Safety inside your own home or wherever you live is fine and well, but you're not at home anymore. I know things have gotten hard for you. They'll probably get harder before you feel safe again."

"I'm starting to figure that out."

The detective pulled her backpack on to her chest. She used both hands to open it. She gave Dar the adjustable, detachable holster containing her semiautomatic pistol.

"Put that on inside the fold of your vest. It'll be uncomfortable for a while. Might take you a few days to get the hang of it. Anyone who looks at you can see that you're armed. Let them guess about the rest."

Dar opened her vest. She unrolled the holster and positioned it under her left arm. "That is uncomfortable."

Bellamy handed over all three loaded clips and the remaining bullets. "Put those in one of your outside pockets. The idea is to reload without hunting for them."

"I know how to do this!"

The older woman remained placid. “Everyone who grows up on a farm thinks they know everything there is to know about guns. The last time I checked, cows, pigs, and chickens don’t shoot back. People do.”

“We don’t shoot chickens!” Dar protested petulantly from lack of sleep.

Bellamy waited for Dar to stow her gun and ammo. “Look around. Whaddya see?”

Dar put the box of bullets in her pack and zipped it shut. “People. Lots of them.”

“They’re getting on with their lives,” the officer commented as Dar closed her vest, “Some of them have already survived worse things than you did. They are moving on, which is what you need to do.”

“What do you know about losing family?”

Bellamy softened. “We see it all the time. Too often, really. The Taggerts and others like them do make a lot of trouble out here. They don’t have so much juice inside.”

Dar was cynical. “Behind your walls? I saw one of them walking around in there. He looked right at me!”

The officer looked at her watch again. “Come on, let’s go. I’m sure they already started boarding. I don’t expect you to believe me, not right now. Take my word for it, there is a difference between what goes on here and what happens inside the enclave. Considering the circumstances, it’s the best we can do.”

Dar accepted the matter-of-fact explanation without voicing more of her resentment. A part of her noticed that she was more acutely aware of the knife and gun in her vest than she had been. She followed Bellamy through the crowds, toward the train platform. Gentle, warm rain fell, soaking them both by the time they reached the wide loading area. Standing in a line to board the rusty, dented passenger car gave her unwanted time to contemplate the difference between justice and revenge.

Original seating in the rail carriage had long since been replaced by wooden benches that were bolted to the floor. Bellamy selected a seat near the middle of the car. She motioned for Dar to be near the window. They sat with their backpacks between them, deliberately taking up the whole bench.

A young man dressed in threadbare flannel approached. "Would you mind if I—"

Bellamy peeled back a flap on her vest to let him see her badge. "Actually, I do."

"Okay," he mumbled, moving on.

Dar pushed her glasses back into place. The increasing odor of unwashed bodies was more noticeable as she looked out the window. Something was happening on or near the platform. "What is that?"

Bellamy tried to lean closer. She pointed casually at several uniformed police officers who were all wearing rain gear. "There, there, and there. That's what real law and order looks like. Just a little something to keep the Taggerts honest while we get on our way."

CHAPTER TEN

Captain Drake muscled his way through the gathering crowd. He approached two of his officers and a big group of rough men carrying an assortment of firearms and rucksacks. He wiped a line of condensation off the brim of his cap. "Is that all of them?"

Officer Monroe enthusiastically elbowed his way past a very glum Frank. "This is our old buddy Frank," he mocked while flicking rain off his coat. "You remember Frank, don't you, Captain? He's got six friends with him today. I didn't know anyone could like him that much."

"He's not alone," Drake decided. "Has anyone seen Ben, or Sorel for that matter?"

Monroe shook his head. "Hey, Frank!" he warned, 'Don't bother turning around. There are three more badges back there. All of you are being detained for questioning. Anyone who can tell me where a Taggert is will not spend the night in our lovely jail."

Frank rubbed his bearded chin, then shifted his wet, floppy hat to stop water flowing down his neck. "I already told you, it's just me and my friends. We're going to Delphi. Train beats walking, so here we are."

Behind them, just yards away, the train started to move after a loud clanging noise rang out. The overworked locomotive, a rusty freight carriage, and three decrepit passenger cars rolled slowly forward. Within minutes, they'd be out of sight.

Officer Hicks pushed his way in close to Drake. "The ticket taker said he took Ben's token and two more. They got on before we arrived"

"That's too bad. Nothing we can do about it now," Drake declared in a low voice. "Disarm these jokers and hold them in the stockade outside the walls. Usual questions. Don't let them go until sundown."

Hicks scowled at the departing train.

"Any takers?" Monroe asked loudly. "The Taggerts pay you. Somebody must know where one of them is. Anyone?"

"Not one word!" Frank shouted. "Everybody stay cool. Nobody is in trouble—yet! You got us, Captain. Can't we settle this with a fine? I got places to be, things to do."

Drake was openly dubious. "No doubt. Problem is, I like to talk. Always have. It's a bad habit that often rubs off on my officers. I'm sure they'd like to hear whatever all of you might have to say. Wouldn't surprise me one bit if our chat with you and your fellow travelers ends up taking all day."

* * *

Ben Taggert straightened the collar of his leather jacket while he watched the enclave fade from sight. He looked over his shoulder at Buck and Zeke. The train had been under way for nearly half an hour. Long enough for his quarry to fall asleep or do something else just as careless. The trio huddled in the back of the last passenger car at the end of the train. "Where's Moe?"

Zeke brushed hot dog crumbs off his coat. "He chickened out. Ran when the cops got close to the train. I think he's been arrested in Belmore a few times. Probably didn't want to get a third strike—if he still has one coming."

Ben turned his back to the small, dust-fogged window set into the carriage door. "Can't blame him for that."

He peered through the dim, hazy interior of the shuddering carriage, evaluating the passengers he could see and his options.

"All right. Okay then," he mused. "We are just more paying passengers. Follow me. I'm going to work my way to the front of this train. We go all the way up to the engineer if we have to. Play the rest by ear."

"What if she's not alone?" Buck wanted to know.

Ben nodded when he saw Zeke scowl. "Right. Doesn't really matter who she's with."

They opened their packs. Each man took several minutes to load their weapons and arm themselves with various blades. All three carried short-barreled pump shotguns. Ben unrolled a light antiballistic vest. He put the body armor on over his shirt, under his leather jacket. There was no point in taking chances. Belmore cops were known to practice loading and firing handguns at least once a week on an outdoor shooting range.

They piled the discarded rucksacks in a corner when their coat pockets were full. Nearby passengers knew who Ben Taggert was. They studiously ignored him. Men and women chatted with each other. Parents attended to their children.

Ben approached the uniformed brakeman, who was pretending to be somewhere else. "Excuse me."

He looked at Ben without making eye contact. "Yes, sir, Mr. Taggert?"

"Is there one of you in every car?" Ben asked.

"Yes, sir," the brakeman affirmed calmly. "Electrical controls don't work anymore. Nobody can fix them. So, we work the brakes in each car when the engine signals."

Ben looked at his henchmen, then at the brakeman. "Do me a favor," he asked the man after some thought. "Pass the word to everyone who works on this train.

Tell them we're here. I'm looking for one of your passengers. I'd appreciate it if, no matter what happens, all of you would just stay out of my way."

The brakeman nodded solemnly. He'd seen this kind of thing before. "I'll see to it."

"One more thing," Ben interjected before the man could move. "We might need to signal the train to stop. How would I do that?"

The brakeman pointed to a long cord suspended over the passenger windows on each side of the car. "Just pull that cord and it rings a bell in the cab. The engineer will stop on a safe section of track. You might not get off where you want, but the train will stop."

Ben thanked the man as he went out of the car. He then prepared himself to follow. "Are you guys ready? We are going into the next passenger car, see? Just follow me. Nobody pulls a knife or a gun until you see me do it first. I mean it. Keep your eyes open. We are not train robbers!"

* * *

Dar looked at her watch. "This is a little more interesting than I thought it would be. I see people sleeping. How can they do that with all the rocking back and forth?"

Bellamy shrugged. "It's all in what you're used to. This run isn't quite twenty miles. Before the Collapse, people rode trains every day that went ten times that far or more. As slow as this old thing is, it beats walking."

Dar agreed. "We'll be there in time for lunch!"

"Depends on how many stops we make," Bellamy warned.

Dar was unconcerned. "Takes me two hours to milk Gerry and scoop up after her. Well, it did. Two hours is no big deal."

The observant detective looked over her shoulder when the brakeman entered the car. "You never know," she said just to keep the small talk going. "Bad guys are like cattle. They make plenty of mess. Especially when you don't want them to."

"You know it!" Dar snickered without taking her eyes off the window and the rolling countryside that came and went.

Bellamy watched him bend over and speak to a similarly dressed man. Both of them looked right at her. She motioned for the standing man to come closer.

He approached. "Excuse me, miss?"

"Can I help you?"

He looked over his shoulder, toward the back of the train. "My friend over there said he recognized you. Are you a police officer?"

Bellamy revealed her badge to him. "Ah," he paused in visible conflict, "I, um— we've got Taggerts onboard."

Dar's jaw dropped, she was no longer interested in the forested land that rolled by.

"How many?" Bellamy asked.

"One. Just one," the railroad employee assured her with some recovered dignity. "With two hired guns."

Bellamy shifted on the bench. "That would be Ben Taggert. Am I right?"

The man nodded competently. "Yes, that's him. He and his associates—"

"Doesn't matter," Bellamy cut him off. "Do me a favor and lock the door to this car."

"I—"

She leaned closer. "*You* can lock the door, or *I'll* get up and do it. Those men are stone cold killers. The worst kind. You know what I mean?"

"Why are they here?" he inquired tentatively.

She turned again, straining to look at the frightened young woman who sat next to her. "You want to tell him, or should I?"

"They killed my whole family!" Dar exclaimed.

The brakeman gestured to his co-worker. The seated man reached out with one hand to lock the door into the passenger carriage. "That won't stop them for very long," he told Bellamy without moving from his seat.

The detective looked at her watch. "Doesn't have to," she mused while looking over Dar's shoulder, out the window. "There's a big baggage car between us and the engine. Is there any way we can get in to it?"

"No," the seated man informed her. "Side doors only. Those are chained and locked before we move. Only the engineer has the key. Don't even think about climbing over it. No ladders. None of the cars on this train have ladders on them, not anymore. They were all cut off years ago. Makes us harder to rob!"

Bellamy regarded Dar with a sour grin. "So, how do you like the train ride so far?"

Dar didn't want to sound ungrateful. "Okay. I wouldn't want to do this all the time."

The officer stood up so she could get a better look at the other passengers, who were looking at her with growing concern. She leaned in close to Dar. "Don't make a scene," she whispered. "I know more about Ben Taggert than I want to. He won't hesitate to use his gun inside this car. When he gets here, you and I have got to go!"

"Where?"

Bellamy moved so Dar could see the carriage door close to the rumbling baggage car. "Keep your voice down!" she admonished. "We wait until they're coming into this car, then we go out the other door and jump off the train."

"That's crazy!"

Tree branches bounced off the carriage window, making Dar jump.

"Calm down," Bellamy urged in her low voice.

"Easy for you to say. I've never—"

The detective put a hand on her charge. "Neither have I! It's not something I put on my list of things do, but here we are! Calm down. You're scaring the other passengers! This is up to you and me. We get out of here and Taggert has no reason to hurt them."

Dar looked at the worried faces staring back at her from around the passenger car. "It's going to be okay," she told them resolutely. "I, um— This is my problem. I'll be taking it with me in just a few minutes. I think. Maybe. You're all going to be fine!"

The inquisitive brakeman sat nervously near his colleague. They tried halfheartedly to calm the people around them.

Bellamy sat. "Get your things together."

Dar focused on her personal effects. She opened her vest.

"Not yet," Bellamy advised evenly. "No guns in here. Just sit still. Every minute they waste back there gets us a little closer to Delphi. Have you ever been in these woods?"

"Never been this far west," Dar admitted.

The officer put her backpack on. "I've seen a few old maps. Parts of them, anyway. Some or all of this area used to be a park or something like that. Don't ask me. I don't know. Seems a little extravagant to have such a big park."

Dar stood up to shrug in to her pack. "Wilderness, wild land, or something like that. Yeah, the word was 'wilderness.' I've seen it in a book recently."

Bellamy got to her feet. "I never have been able to find enough spare time to read." She raised her voice at the two nearby brakemen. "Hey, you! Do me a favor and ask these people to move back into your half of this car!"

The railroad man who was still standing began to wave frantically at the passengers. "Come on, everyone! This way, please! That woman is a police officer and we need to get out of her way. Come on, let's go. Taggerts are going to be here any minute!"

Bellamy stood up. She put a hand on Dar's shoulder. "So. They're going to come in back there, through all those people. Let's you and me go stand up front. Over there, away from everyone who doesn't want to get shot."

* * *

Ben Taggert was trying to lead the way. The brakeman in the second passenger car knew who he was, which didn't seem to help. All of the passengers had some kind of luggage, most of which was piled near seats or in the aisle.

"Excuse me, please. Coming through!"

As forewarned as the brake operator was supposed to be, he didn't seem to care about Ben's need for speed. "Please, sir! These are the most honest and hard-working people. Not one of them is a criminal! We don't let that type on our train!"

Knowing that Zeke and Buck would follow his lead, Ben slowed his pace and resisted the temptation to draw his pistol. The Taggert name wasn't always appreciated outside the walls of the Tumwater enclave, where the extended family ruled without competition. When it was, that respect tended to be obsequious, which made it almost impossible for him to tell if their admiration was real or fake.

No matter what any of these people on this train thought about him, his need for finesse was quite real. A third glance satisfied him that his quarry wasn't in this car. "Sorry to bother you. We'll be moving along. Have a good day!"

Cool, bracing wind hit him in the face when he opened the door between carriages. He stepped from one platform, over the hitch, to the balcony of the last passenger car. His hat flew away as he looked through the small window in the door.

"She's in there!" he shouted into the wind.

Buck and Zeke looked questioningly at him. Ben swore and went back into the jostling passenger car. "Shotguns!" he demanded when he was out of the wind. "Buck goes first. Zeke, you follow me. They've done us the favor of getting away from the passengers. Soon as you get in there, kill 'em!"

* * *

Dar took off her glasses and put them into a vest pocket. She had just enough time to secure the pocket with a sticky tab. The rear door of the undulating passenger car was blown apart by several sudden shotgun blasts. Men, women, and children screamed as they were pelted by a random spray of low-velocity lead pellets.

Detective Bellamy yanked open the front door of the passenger car. She pushed Dar through, onto the narrow platform balcony. "Go, go, go!"

Without her glasses, Dar was instinctively paralyzed by spears of flickering sunlight stabbing through the rippling pattern of blurry trees that changed as fast as the train moved. Two rapid gunshots rang out behind her. They were answered by a pair of shotgun blasts. Dar closed her eyes and jumped. Her frantic leap propelled her outward and away from the rolling train.

Twenty years earlier, tired, hungry workers who had labored for many weeks to build the section of salvaged track she now fled from had made a logistical choice based on their dwindling resources. They had cleared very little land on either side of the track they laid because they were almost out of food, water, wages, and useful tools to chop down trees. In the years that followed, area residents had carved out small, visible clearings near the tracks when they wanted the train to stop.

None of those decisions had much impact on the day-to-day activity of the railroad. As Dar began her plunge from the train, that necessity-driven outcome altered her future. In her rush to get off the train, she didn't bother to look for an opening in the tree line. Even if she had been able to see a gap in the foliage before the train passed it, she would have been hard-pressed to time her leap accordingly.

Dar slammed in to a tree just as her feet began to touch the ground. She blacked out.

CHAPTER ELEVEN

Dar woke face down in tall, sharp-edged grass; dead leaves; and lots of crawling insects. A flurry of loud gunshots nearby sent a surge of adrenaline through her. Some part of her knew they were pistol shots. She thrashed through the undergrowth in an uncoordinated effort to stand as more gunshots echoed through the trees. Flailing her arms and legs, she scuttled on her hands and knees for several seconds, clawing her way to a spruce trunk that she used for leverage to stand.

Somewhere close by, a man's voice screamed out in raw agony. Dar forced herself to take a deep breath and hold it. She closed her eyes while the sound of hurried footfalls and breaking branches faded. Feeling a need to breathe, she exhaled, took another breath, and opened her eyes. Trees and bushes came back into focus as her lungs filled. Steadiness returned. She was looking at her booted feet when another gunshot made her swear.

Dar staggered away from the tree. She put on her glasses and slowly looked around. Narrow game trails—the kind made by rabbits and other small creatures—were visible between many of the needle-bearing trees. Sights and sounds of the forest were familiar. They reminded Dar of countless hunting trips with her family.

She picked her way through or around stands of trees while trying to remember what direction the gunfire had come from. Distant, angry voices made her skin crawl when she was close enough to realize what they were. Slowly drawing her semiautomatic pistol, she flicked off the safety and worked the slide to chamber a round. Placing her thumb on the hammer, she drew it back with a soft click. Walking deliberately, she crouched to silently enter a thicket of bushes.

The blurry silhouette of a standing person coalesced when she got close enough to see past individual branches and layers of green leaves. As angry and amped up as she was, what she observed was enough to make her hesitate.

* * *

Ben Taggert struggled to rein in his anger. More than ever, he needed to be calm. He kept his smoking hot pistol pointed at the bleeding woman who had been forced to kneel on the ground in front of him. His chest ached from the reduced impact of her bullets, many of which had been fired from medium or long ranges.

“I really don’t blame you for killing Zeke on the train,” he swore through his pain. “He always was too eager.”

Bellamy sat without comment. Ben nudged her with the toe of his boot to indicate the splayed corpse of Buck, flat on his back, covered in blood. “That, on the other hand, I do blame you for! Who knows? You might’ve pulled this off if you had more ammo.”

“Let’s just get this over with.”

Ben walked slowly around his prisoner, careful to stay out of her reach. His eyes roamed over what he saw without any appreciation. He’d always hated being in the woods, even when those miserable moments were part of a family outing.

“Tell me where she is. That’s all I want to know, and we’re finished.”

“Don’t know.”

Ben stopped roaming. He stood with his back to Dar. "I could believe it, if you weren't so eager to just sit there and bleed out."

Bellamy looked up at him emotionlessly. Tiny hairs on the back of her neck bristled while she focused her contempt. Despite the disorienting pain of several gunshot wounds and waning vigor from blood loss, she did know—*she wasn't alone*.

Ben reprimanded her with a wave of his gun. "That hero thing doesn't work on me. I know your kind. Seen enough like you to know that no amount of hot lead or cold steel in your guts is enough to make you see things our way. So, you can have this quick, or I'll just leave you out here for whatever likes to snack after dark."

Experience and skill made Bellamy intuitively aware of a swaying bush behind Ben. She forced herself to look away from it. "You're not the outdoorsy type, are you?"

Ben was tired. He swore reflexively. "No, not one bit! I like streets under my feet. Did you know, we've still got computers? You'd be amazed if you could see what those fabricators turn out!"

Bellamy privately hoped the worsening pain she felt wasn't making her hallucinate. If Dar was actually hiding in the nearby bushes close enough to see Ben Taggert clearly, she might be listening for clues. Even if she couldn't see him very well, she could still hear him run his mouth. "I'll be amazed if you'd just shut up and get this over with! I'd rather be dinner for a wolf. It beats having you save bullets by talking me to death!"

Ben lunged closer, flogging Bellamy with the barrel of his pistol. "Where is she?!?"

"Thought so," she sneered while coughing blood. "Y-your gun is empty, am I right?"

Ben stepped away cautiously. He kept his eyes on her while using his free left hand to search the left-side pockets of his leather jacket.

"Yeah." He nodded in grim satisfaction while showing her the full clip. "Thought I had another one. It's all I need to finish you and walk out of here with a margin of safety. If, like you say, what's-her-name isn't here, she'll be running scared all the way to Delphi."

Bellamy feigned indifference. "I can see how you might think that."

Ben surveyed his surroundings one more time. Talking about his lack of ammunition made him feel vulnerable. "Did you tell her to move on out of here?"

"Of course I did!"

Ben's anger slackened. Telling the kid to run was the sort of thing a badge would do. He advanced toward Bellamy from her right side, raising his gun. "I hope it was worth it. Look away and close your eyes."

* * *

Dar stood upright as she stepped out of the bushes. "Stop!"

Ben turned to see her gun pointed at his chest. "You came back?"

"Never went away," she told him, adjusting her aim with both hands.

"*Shoot him*!" Bellamy insisted with all the strength she had left. "H-he's only got one or two bullets left in his clip. He's a lousy shot. He can't get both of us!"

Ben moved to put the prostrate Bellamy between himself and Dar. He'd been in tight spots before; all he had to do was play for time and wait for her to make just one mistake. He looked at the full clip in his hand, then at Dar. "You basically got me, at point-blank. One or two rounds, yeah. Doesn't mean much when we're this close. No matter what you do, she's dead. You might get through my body armor. Then again, you might not!"

"Only one way to find out," Dar interjected, widening her stance.

Ben felt the weight of the clip in his hand. He pointed his pistol at the back of Bellamy's downturned head. "You want to save her and I have unfinished business with you. Looks like a standoff. One of us needs to leave. Why don't you just step back into those bushes and be gone? Leave this territory and you'll never have to see me again or hear the name Taggert for as long as you live."

"Liar!" Bellamy mumbled.

Ben didn't take his gaze off Dar. "Ask anyone. I keep my word. It's a Taggert thing. I am going to catch Hell for not bringing you in. That's okay—as long as you are *gone*!"

Dar took a step closer. "No."

He resisted the urge to retreat. "Hey, come on, now! We are both going to get hurt, no matter how this works out. Tell you what, how about this. What if I—"

Bellamy struggled to lift her head. "No! He's just going to circle back and around. Catch you off guard, get you in your sleep…"

Dar moved half a step to change her angle, allowing her to see more of Ben's profile. The body armor covering his chest was worn in places where it had stopped many bullets. She'd never fired a shot in anger. That fact made her doubt the accuracy of any head shot. "I shoot pigs," she told him. "Greedy, bossy pigs get shot first because they make life hard for the others. Put your gun down. She can take you in. I'll swear out the complaint."

Ben was incredulous. "I know you're wearing glasses. Can't you see she's gut shot? Nobody lives through that without a doctor!"

Dar licked her drying lips. "She dies, you die."

"Okay," he relented while raising both of his arms up high. "Look. Somebody needs to make a show of good faith. Might as well be me. So, here I go!"

He ejected the magazine from his gun and kicked it away when it fell to the ground. "See? No bullets! Empty gun. Now, what are you going to do?"

"Drop the other clip," she demanded.

"This?" he gestured at the full mag in his hand. "No, I need this. Nobody comes in or goes out of these woods without protecting themselves. That's just what I'm going to do, with or without any good faith on your part. I'm leaving!"

Bellamy was unable to move. "Don't…"

Ben turned on his heel. Dar followed him pace for pace with her weapon trained on his back until she was able to shield Bellamy with her own body.

With practiced ease, Ben slid the full clip into the receiver of his semiauto pistol. "Do me a favor," he asked while working the slide. "Don't tell anyone you had a gun on me. It would be bad for my reputation."

Dar tensed when she heard his magazine lock in. "Don't do it!"

He turned suddenly, surprised to see her so close. His thumb cocked the hammer as his wrist rotated to aim the gun. "You won't—"

Dar fired. Ben staggered backward with the force of each bullet that struck his chest. Advancing with each pull of her trigger, she drove him back nine times before her gun was empty. The white-hot barrel smoked when the retracted slide action remained open. Ben fell onto his back with an astonished look on his face.

She kicked him while she reloaded. "Why did you make me do it?"

Some effort was needed to cock the hot handgun. She held the pistol with one hand while her most affected fingers tingled with pain. "Lousy bastard! Why?"

There was no doubt about his demise. Ben Taggert was very dead. His body armor was shredded in three different places on his chest and abdomen. Dark blood streamed down his sides, pooling inside the folds of his leather jacket.

Dar kicked his handgun away before turning to Bellamy.

"He's gone," she said softly while reloading and holstering her gun. She knelt next to the dying woman.

Bellamy leaned on Dar. "Thought so. It's not your fault. Not sure if I would have just let him walk away."

"You would've let him go," Dar assured with a hug. "There's a part of me that didn't want him to go. How did I know he was going to try something?"

Bellamy's voice was hard to hear. "You have good instincts. They saved you 'n me. Problem is, you've got to finish what you started."

"How?"

The mortally wounded woman slumped. "Over that way, a few paces beyond Buck. Find my rucksack and bring it to me."

Dar eased Bellamy on to her back. "Might as well be comfortable," she said, straightening the officer's legs.

She hunted for Bellamy's backpack for several seconds. Finding it, she brought it to the reclining detective. "Here you go," she smiled while taking off her own pack and sitting on the trampled grass.

Bellamy laid the pack on her chest. She used both bloodstained hands to open it. Rummaging for a small pad of paper and a ballpoint ink pen, she put the pack aside before scribbling a note. "When I'm done, I want you to take this to the cops in Delphi."

"We need to get some bandages on you!"

"Knock it off!" Bellamy snapped. "If you didn't already know what death looks like, you do now."

"I didn't—"

"Nobody with a conscience does—ever," Bellamy empathized while she kept writing. "Something inside you is messed up if you want to go looking for violence or you want to kill for the sake of just doing it. The Taggerts of this world have always wanted to solve most problems with violence. They think obedience is the same as law and order. It's not. Fear is always intended to make you comply. Freedom is hard to explain, and harder to keep, because you might have to fight back against what causes that fear."

"I—"

"One minute!" Bellamy chided hoarsely. "Please, just give me a minute. It's getting hard for my eyes to focus. I don't usually write reports in situations like this. Being shot is new for me. I can't recommend it."

She let the pen and pad of paper fall out of her hands, onto the ground, after finishing the carefully worded note. "Take that page. Put it deep inside one of your good pockets."

Dar tore the page off the pad, folding it. "I'm sorry."

"Nah," Bellamy sighed with her eyes closed. "You didn't do this. It's not your fault. You should be glad. One of the meaner pigs isn't around any longer. He won't hurt anyone. Not anymore. A day or so in the forest should be no problem for a farm girl. You'll work harder to get past Sorel. He's waiting for you near the school."

"I know."

Bellamy kept her eyes closed. "Stay off the tracks if you can. You can't always hear the train coming. Nobody knows for sure what's out here. Might be woods; might be more. Play it safe. Avoid people as much as you can. Stay off cleared land. Avoid anything that looks like a farm or a homestead. If you can hear voices or livestock, you're too close. They won't hesitate to hand you over to the Taggerts. Got it?"

Dar cringed at the sight of Bellamy's heaving chest. "Yeah, I got it. Sounds a lot like what my parents told me and Jack. If it's not yours, stay off or leave it alone."

She slid the folded page into one her largest interior vest pockets as Bellamy reached with a trembling hand to unclip her bloodstained badge. She held it out for Dar to take. "I know it's a lot to ask, but—if you would, put this with the piece of paper I gave you. Give both of them to the authorities in Delphi."

"What—"

Bellamy coughed blood. "Yeah. They don't like the Taggerts any more than you do. Nobody with that last name will be welcome inside the walls of their enclave. Not when word gets out about how they killed a cop."

Dar cupped the badge in her hand, softly wiping smears of blood on her shirt sleeve. She inserted it into the protected pocket containing the note just as Bellamy expired.

Frustration welled up inside her. She pounded her fist on the ground. Working through her tears, she forced herself to stand and look around. Her wristwatch agreed with the early afternoon sun; it was just after 2 p.m. when she finished pulling herself together.

Bellamy's backpack was full of surprises that included a sturdy folding metal shovel. Dar felt guilty about going through the personal effects of somebody she knew, even if that association had been brief. She ignored the remaining contents, instead focusing on the shovel. It unfolded easily. The short length of it balanced effortlessly in her hands.

"Amazing."

Searching Buck's blood soaked body was as unpleasant as she had thought it would be. "Ew," she complained while extracting unspent shotgun shells from his soggy pockets.

Ben's fallen corpse was not any easier for her grapple with. He stank of open bowels. "Why am I not surprised? You were definitely full of it."

The pockets of Ben's leather jacket contained beef jerky, chewing gum, and dozens of loose pistol bullets. Dar spent nearly an hour finding good places in her vest and pack for what she was taking. The nature of what she was doing made her think about Marsh and what he'd said about his own past as a scavenger.

Dar looked at her watch again, then at the pair of empty, short-barreled pump shotguns on the ground near the earth mound covering Bellamy. "I would leave one of those for you, but somehow, I don't think you need it."

She picked up one of the shotguns and threw it into the nearby bushes. Reaching for the remaining weapon, she jammed it into a canvas strap on her own rucksack. Bellamy's pack came next, easily mashed on top of what she was already carrying.

"Okay then." She double-checked herself. "Let's have a look at the compass and find out which way to go."

She reached into the pocket where she knew it was. Her hand filled with broken parts. The casing and what was left of the internal workings rolled in the palm of her dirty hand. Aching deep inside her chest was an unwanted reminder of the tree she'd slammed into. "After stupidly jumping off the damned train!"

CHAPTER TWELVE

Dar threw away the pieces of her broken compass. She wasn't concerned about the loss of the navigation aid, even if the reason for it was embarrassing. "Good thing I've got a spare," she told herself while unwrapping a piece of chewing gum.

Adjusting her load and her glasses, Dar watched the sky intently. "Sun rises in the east, which is that way. Sun sets in the west, which is over there. Delphi is west, so—we go that way!"

She walked casually through the forest while absent-mindedly chomping on a wad of old, but flavorful, gum. The experience was strangely relaxing. She could almost make herself believe the events of the last few hours hadn't happened. "But they did," she confessed to the wilderness.

Minutes passed. Her booted feet forced their way through dense patches of weeds. She slowed and stopped when she saw that the trees nearby were unusually far apart. Getting closer, she could see patches of moss-covered asphalt between scattered bushes and swaths of grass. From past experience, she knew she was looking at remnants of a pre-Collapse road. Curiosity motivated her to stand on the uneven artificial surface.

Drawing on what was common knowledge, she observed how the road appeared to run east to west, in approximately the same direction she was going. "Why do I think that's not a coincidence?"

Dar remembered what some of the passengers had talked about when they looked out the windows of the moving train. Somewhere behind her was a wooden trestle big enough to support the train when it crossed over the Black River. Nobody had said anything that she could recall about old roads.

Blue sky and sun made the walk pleasant, she continued on what remained of the road. As she walked, Dar remembered a few of the things her grandparents had said about a scenic drive. The idea of just getting in a car and rolling down the road seemed weird. "Even if I wanted to do that, where would I find the time?"

Drinking from her water bottle, she ate strips of jerky as the miles went slowly by. Long shadows slowed her progress when the sun slipped down below the distant horizon. The shape of a road sign that was still standing got her attention. She walked right up to it. Red rust showed through what had been green paint and silver-white reflective lettering. "Evergreen Beach, Haven Site, ten miles," she read out loud.

Dar took off her glasses and rubbed her eyes. Getting closer to squint in the gloom, she read the sign again. "H-a-v-e-n, S-i-t-e. That says Haven, or I'm losing my mind!"

She looked back in the direction she'd come from. Sounds of animal life around her seemed suddenly menacing. Touching the sign caused some of the lettering to flake off. Feeling the paint give way made her uneasy.

A glance upward, through the canopy of trees, confirmed that she had less than an hour of daylight left to find shelter. Walking around the sign, she strained to see in every direction. She was able to pick out trees, bushes, and descending gloom.

She imagined that what she saw had once been a carefully planned two-lane highway, possibly constructed by hundreds, or even thousands, of robots that were led by a handful of skilled human engineers.

"Okay," she surmised to herself. "So, I build a road through a forest because I don't want anyone to mess it up. Why would I put a sign right here?"

Dar struggled to remember something—anything—useful about pre-Collapse lore. Factoids from the pages of Helen's tattered textbooks raced through her troubled mind. None of them seemed relatable to a person who was lost in the woods.

She touched the edge of the sign. "I'm here. If I go this way, I eventually get there—to Evergreen Beach and the Haven Site. Hm. I might put a sign here if I wanted people to be sure this was the right way to go. That must mean there is a turnoff around here somewhere. A road that takes you someplace else."

The logic wasn't much to go on, though it was enough inspiration to make Dar walk until she had to use a flashlight to follow the ruined road. Two miles past the road sign, she was rewarded with what had been the highway turnoff. Rusty guard rails outlined what was once a sloping northward turn in the pavement. Corroded carcasses of stripped automobiles were overgrown with greenery. She walked past them without much thought.

Nestled among the trees, she found a sheltered automated charging station that had once powered millions of electric cars. The bright orange structure was hard to miss. Parts of it gleamed in the beam of her light. She reconsidered the wrecks she had just walked by.

Swinging her flashlight left and right, she stopped to draw her gun and make it ready before approaching a tall, slim, touch screen equipped kiosk that was labeled 'Ask Me.'

Dar tapped the cold metal surface of the single-story building with the illuminated tip of her flashlight. Cars, trucks, and vans were nothing new to Dar. She'd seen them used by her neighbors. From six years of homeschooling, Dar knew the oldest automobiles ran on gasoline. Charging stations like the one she stood in were converted gas stations. Gasoline-powered transport had become a thing of the past by the mid-21st Century.

She played her beam over the high metal canopy over her head. Over her shoulder, she saw a trio of charging stations, each waiting for customers who might never come. Beyond them, a nondescript row of cannibalized cars was hard to see in the fading light.

"If I remember correctly, these things usually have a bathroom and a snack machine."

The nearby kiosk lit up. A smiling cartoon face appeared on the dust-covered screen. "I'm sorry, we are temporarily unable to service your vehicle!" it apologized too loudly. "You'll have to come back later."

Dar jumped with fright. She laughed at herself when she realized she had almost shot the interactive display. "Can I at least use the bathroom?" she joked.

The animated face seemed friendly enough. Its volume lowered. "Yes, of course! You'll find our facility on the side of this building. Use your customer pass to enter. Please let me know if you have any more questions."

"What about the snack machine?"

The image flickered, then moped. "I don't think we have one."

Dar was amused by the pitiable performance of the display. She couldn't resist the temptation to be just a little antagonistic. "What about some juice for my car?"

The apologetic image responded cheerfully, "I'm sorry, we are temporarily unable to service your vehicle."

Dar laughed until her stomach hurt. "C-can you tell me how I get to Haven?"

The energetic image seemed to think. "Continue west for seven-point-five miles, then turn off at the Evergreen Beach Club. The nearest Haven Site occupies that same location. Please be sure to have your identification ready before you arrive or go inside."

Two minutes later, Dar found the unisex bathroom on the other side of the building. Aiming her handgun carefully from a safe distance, she fired into the lock three times before the door swung open. Bright white interior lighting came on when she entered.

"What is your gender preference?" a mechanical voice asked from the ceiling.

Dar did a double-take at herself in the reflection of a small mirror on the nearest wall. "I like boys, if that's what you're asking."

"Thank you," the voice replied as a powered hygiene unit mounted on the back wall configured itself as a urinal.

She laughed. "I'm a girl—woman, I mean. Give me the other thing!"

The overhead voice softly apologized. The urinal silently transformed into a toilet. "Warning, the door to this facility is not properly closed."

Ignoring the voice, Dar used the toilet. The mechanism was similar enough to others that she had used that she had no difficulties in operating it.

Once she was finished, Dar leaned out into the evening air. She spat out her used chewing gum before closing the door. "Warning," the overhead voice announced, "The door to this facility is not properly closed."

Dar eyed the bullet holes in the locking mechanism while holstering her handgun. One of the spent bullets she'd fired was on the hard plastic floor between her feet. A quick search of the restroom was enough to find the other two flattened slugs. She rapped her bare knuckles on one of the sturdy gray walls. "Bullet-proof bathroom!" she giggled. "I know where I'm sleeping!"

Sitting on the cool, clean floor, Dar put her back to one wall to be more comfortable. With both of her feet wedged against the damaged door, she was fast asleep in minutes despite the overhead lighting.

Vivid fragments of the last few days swirled through her unconscious mind. The agony of losing her family was briefly overshadowed by feelings of guilt. She would always regret her inability to save them.

Grief gave way to curiosity when she entered the deepest, most restful phase of sleep. Unchained imagination allowed her to relive every moment she could still remember from the times when the subject of Haven was a topic of good-natured speculative conversation among family and friends, or when she had actually seen some circumstantial evidence of its existence.

* * *

Dar remembered her last exam with Helen. She put down her pencil to drink from a small glass of cold water. Using her free hand to turn a page in one of the old textbooks, she was able to make out the start of a new chapter.

"Helen?"

"Yes," the woman nodded with some anticipation.

Dar put her finger on the page. "Why do most people think Haven is just one place? Says here, there were supposed to be thousands of 'designated locations.' All of them were set up by governments and corporations, to provide food, water, and shelter for what they called 'displaced people.' If that's true, then why—"

Helen clearly had some regrets. "No matter how hard we try, none of us remember everything that's in those books. I used to have hundreds of them. Now, all I have left is what's in my saddle bags and what's in storage back at the school in Delphi. All of that boils down to just one thing. Most people are not hearing about the past, so they don't really know much about it."

Dar remembered turning the page, which felt limp and dry. "I can't imagine anyone would want—"

"Don't jump to conclusions," Helen reprimanded. "The average person learns what they need to know. It's easy to be unaware of things when the people around you are in the same boat. Especially when you trust them."

Dar wished she could interpret Helen's blurry expression. "Even if the truth has been lost over time, why do so many people talk about Haven like it's just one place?"

The older woman chuckled. "It's called 'folklore.' You can think of it as a form of mythology. Knowledge fragments over time. People lose track of the simplest truth."

Dar felt more at ease. "So. It's not true? There is no Haven?"

Helen placed her weathered hands on the table in a way that gave her time to think. "Concepts remain with us for as long as most of us like them. One generation tells the next, and so on. The idea of Haven is still with us, even if we don't recall what it was."

Dar woke slowly with new confidence. "I want to believe."

* * *

She opened the door of the small restroom to see the sun was already up. Her watch told her it was 7:30 a.m. Seeing the lavatory with fresh eyes, she marveled at the efficient interior. A small sink provided warm or cool water that didn't smell bad, so she drank some and used more to wipe some of the grime off her arms, hands, face, and neck. A quick scrub and a change of socks made her feet feel refreshed and ready for another day of long-distance walking.

Drawing tepid water from the sink, she mixed up a freeze-dried meal and ate it from the container pouch it had been packed in, using a metal spork. Sitting on the toilet with the lid down, she read small print on the pouch. "'Fauxvaca with Egg Noodles and Sauce. Fabricated meat product, ideal for human consumption.' Well, that's a matter of opinion."

Tying her boot laces, Dar realized the overhead light was still on. "What time is it?"

"8:15 a.m.," the machine voice told her.

"There's daylight out there," Dar stated obviously. "Why is the light still on?"

"The door is ajar," she was told by the mechanical voice.

Dar was perturbed. "Thank you."

"You are welcome."

* * *

Minutes later, she closed the door to the restroom. Breathing in the crisp morning air, she fumbled for the spare compass in her father's rucksack. Holding it in her hand, she pressed the button labeled "seek." The displayed indicator swerved, then pointed west. She turned in the general direction of what she thought was north, based on the position of the sun. The needle stubbornly pointed west.

Dar took off her glasses to have a closer look at the gadget. Turning it over in her hand, she was able to make out small, raised lettering. "Property of U.S. Government."

She scratched her head and put her glasses back on. "Must be broken," she decided before putting the gadget in a vest pocket.

Indulging herself with more chewing gum, Dar drank from her water bottle while she walked around trees and bushes growing up through the asphalt of the moss-covered road. As the day wore on, she began to understand why nobody lived in such a remote place. Beyond the boundaries of the neglected roadway, high bushes and tall grass competed with copses of trees for sunlight. "This must've been what they meant by 'boondocks,'" she decided, swatting away a mosquito.

Shouldering her two-pack load was starting to be uncomfortable when she got near the rusty remains of a police car, abandoned by the side of the road. A shield-style logo was visible on the driver's side door. "State Trooper," she made out from what was left of the faded, peeling decal.

On a whim, she pulled out the compass gadget to have another look at it. The needle swung unsteadily in a northeasterly direction. "Make up your mind!" she complained while pushing the seek button.

Dar kept on walking. She had just about lost interest in the gadget when she saw something large that appeared to be blocking the road ahead. Slowing her pace, she put the unfamiliar object back in to her pocket. A memory stirred when she got close enough to make out the shape of treads instead of wheels. "Military vehicle," she recalled from one of Helen's textbooks.

Whatever it had been, it was still huge. She was amazed by the size of the turret and what was left of the main gun. Round metal doors hung open on the left and right sides. A ramp on the rear was down, revealing a cavernous, fire-damaged interior containing what looked like reinforced metal seating for two dozen people.

Dar was tempted to go poking around inside for loot. There was no way to know what she might find. Advice given to her by her parents many times counseled against searching military vehicles because they might be booby trapped.

She tried using her flashlight to probe the interior. There was too much daylight to effectively see the beam.

She reluctantly turned away from the rusting hulk while safely stowing her flashlight. Looking left, then right, her eyes adjusted to shifting shadows in the area. She was able to make out parts of a high chain-link fence that were hidden by dense intertwined ferns and thin saplings. The obstruction seemed out of place. Starring at the veiled segments only made each of them more obvious to her.

Dar shuffled along the crumbling shoulder of the road until she was close enough to see the steel strands of the fence. More of the fallen fence was visible to her left, causing her to take a few more steps. "What in the world?"

Small pieces of metal, glass, and plastic crunched nosily under her dirty boots as she passed beyond the fence line. Through a maze of bushes and trees, she could make out several pancaked buildings. All of them had caved in decades earlier.

She drew her gun while approaching the nearest corrugated metal building. A sign was still visible on its crumpled skin. Making the firearm ready in one hand, she used the toe of her left boot to kick away broken branches and dead leaves.

What she saw took her breath away. "U.S. Government, Emergency Relocation Camp."

A combination of rust and gaping bullet holes made the rest of the sign unreadable. Dar knelt to touch the lettering with her free hand. She probed some of the bullet holes with a cautious finger. "This can't be it," she disbelieved. "There has got to be more!"

CHAPTER THIRTEEN

Dar wandered in dazed silence among the ruined structures with her pistol in hand. Midday became afternoon before she was able to compose herself. Everything miserable she had survived over the last four days made the moment she was in feel anticlimactic. Feelings of disappointment deepened to hopelessness and despair when she thought about how much the idea of places like the one she was in meant to anyone who cared enough to keep the cherished dream.

The words of Helen came back to Dar. "One generation tells the next," she muttered to herself. "The idea of Haven is still with us, even if we don't recall what it was."

She stopped in the cold shadow of a flattened building to rest and get her bearings. "Even if we don't recall what it was."

The position of the sun was hard to determine through dense tree cover surrounding the rundown camp. As disappointed as she was, Dar knew she should move on or find a place nearby to spend the night. With some effort, she might find a dry space in one of the ruined structures that would shield her from prying eyes and the weather.

She was starting to feel indecisive when something in a vest pocket began to beep. The unfamiliar sound was just as intriguing as it was frightening. Dar gently probed her pockets with one hand.

The source of the repetitive noise turned out to be the strange, not-so-helpful compass. Avoiding the temptation to holster her gun, she examined the beeping gadget with her back to the demolished building. The instrument's digital dial displayed a large, round, green dot.

She shook the gadget between her fingers. "Yeah. That's not helpful. What are you trying to tell me?"

A single press of the seek button silenced the object. Its compass needle reappeared, pointing northwest. "First west, and now kinda-sorta north. The color of green is usually good on electronics, so I can assume that means something positive."

Turning to her left, she observed the needle make a slight correction. "So, I'm here. Needle pointed west and I went west. I'm here. Now, it seems to want something else."

Dar pondered the purpose of the green dot. "Whatever Haven is or was, this is not it."

She put the gadget away, taking a moment to be sure all the sticky tabs on her vest were secured. A gust of wind blew dead leaves across the ground. Soft animal noises continued around her. Some part of her was now more aware of the abandoned camp than she had been. That new insight inspired her to rethink the purpose of the gadget and its pulsing green dot.

Dar opened her pocket and took out the gadget. Pressing the seek button caused the green dot to appear with a beep. "Yes, I know that!"

The digital compass dial silently took the place of the green dot, pointing northwest.

"I'm glad one of us is happy!" Dar criticized pointedly.

She craned her neck, looking around meticulously to be certain she was still alone. Something wasn't adding up. She started to dislike the mysterious gadget in her hand. "You're not a compass. So, why did my father put you in his bag?"

The urgency of that question made her think about the other unusual items in the bag. The two-page emergency notification, a military document, and the aggravating gadget were somehow connected. Venting her anger, Dar clutched the enigmatic object in her fist, wishing she could squeeze some truth out of it.

Frustration made her feel a twinge of guilt. She opened her sweaty hand contritely.

"I've been running scared. I haven't really been calm long enough to ask many questions. For as long as I can remember, we planned for trouble. Always knew somebody might want to rob us, take what we worked for. Maybe even kill us to get it, if they had to."

Dar raised her hand up to eye level where she could see the gadget in every detail. "This thing, the papers, and the money. They were put in this pack for another purpose."

She closed her eyes. "If I had a bag full of secrets, I would still need to tell somebody about them eventually. You know, just in case something really bad happened to me."

Her empathetic assumption triggered a memory. She recalled her father standing next to a cluttered table in the kitchen, just a few minutes before the family was attacked. He looked right her, speaking casually. "Dar, go to the basement and get my bug-out bag. Bring it to me. There are some things you and Jack need to know before we stand watch."

"Are you sure?" Clare worried.

Henry nodded. "We agreed to tell 'em when Jack was old enough for high school and we didn't. Are we just going to keep putting it off?"

Noisy birds flying overhead jarred Dar back to reality. She opened her eyes in time to see the erratic flock vanish through far away trees.

"What were you going to tell us about this?"

She thought about her mother's maiden name, as it had appeared on the marriage license. "Yeah. Okay, that's a little icky, but it's not Haven. Taggerts would be a lot harder to live with if they knew anything that mattered about—"

Dar halted in speechlessness; the idea was just too monstrous. The gadget in her hand took on a new importance. Her grandfather—

"*You were here*," she shuddered.

The combination of evacuation notice and military discharge now made more sense. Anyone who got one of those, or both, would think they were a big deal. "Keep it like you would hang onto a marriage license or a birth certificate."

She screamed with intense amazement and aggravation. "Why didn't you tell me?"

The answer was painfully obvious. Dar and Jack had been only seconds away from being told the harsh truth about their tenuous connection to the Taggert dynasty—and to whatever Haven was or might still be!

Dar staggered over to a rusty, broken park bench. She sat just as tears began to flow.

"There is nothing to be sorry about," she declared, holstering her handgun. "It was a tough break. Nothing more than bad luck. One more minute ether way probably wouldn't have changed how things turned out, even if we had known."

She released her grip on the gadget and put it away. After a few long, deep breaths, she blew her nose with a handkerchief. Cool afternoon shadows began to creep over grass and weeds. Diminishing daylight made it harder for her to see individual buildings. As somber as the moment was, it wasn't enough to worsen her mood.

Dar stood up. She looked around while wiping her nose.

"It's going to be dark soon."

She shifted her load before going deeper into the camp, toward what she thought would be the center. Some of what she had read in the textbooks Helen provided came back to her while she walked. All refugee camps, like this one, that served people fleeing from major population centers were supposed to be temporary, never permanent. They were made to be put up or taken down rapidly.

Dar stopped near what she thought might've been a planned intersection of footpaths between structures. The presence of so many overgrown, flattened buildings was enough to make her think the camp had been abandoned.

"Something must have happened here. They didn't have time to take it apart."

She was trying to decide which way to go when she was briefly blinded by a passing gleam of sunlight flashing off a glossy surface. She waited calmly for her eyes to adjust. Dar couldn't remember seeing anything reflective or shiny in these woods since she left the charging station.

"All that bright orange and silver. Yeah, they wanted to be noticed! So. What is still here that would be that shiny?"

"Over there," she decided.

Dar imagined how countless looters would have already stripped the camp clean while she worked her way around the nearest building. With her pistol in one hand and a flashlight in the other, she felt her way slowly through a maze of wreckage that blocked her vision.

Sharp, twisted metal poked her uncomfortably several times before she found an opening large enough to shuffle through. In the fading glow of the distant sunset, she was able to see what first appeared to be a silver square on a slow-moving pedestal.

Dar swung her flashlight beam around. "Solar panel," she realized. "What would you be powering in the middle of all this unhappy mess?"

The gadget in her vest pocket beeped. "Be quiet!" she complained, slapping it with a clenched hand. The gadget continued beeping, forcing her to stuff the flashlight into her open mouth so she could use her free hand to reach for the irritating instrument. Tearing open the pocket flap, she grabbed it angrily. Mashing the seek button with her thumb, she sighed when it stopped beeping.

The glowing green dot on the round display caught her eye. "Fine. Good for you! What prize do I get?"

Stepping away from something sharp, Dar's attention was drawn to a green light on the pedestal. In the beam of her flashlight, she could make out tiny letters. "Waypoint," she verbalized. "Way-point. That's like a place you can stop on your way to something, isn't it?"

She swore at the solar panel, half-heartedly kicking the pedestal with her booted foot. "Makes a lot of sense, *if somebody tells you what it is*!"

Dar was trying to bite down on her temper when she tripped over a thick, black cord on the ground. Pointing her flashlight at the spot where it connected to the pedestal, she played her beam over the cluttered group, away from the photovoltaic array, to the side of what had been a large building.

"You're not just a waypoint," she observed logically. "You're actually powering…something."

She clipped the light to her vest before walking closer to the structure. In the glare of her beam, she could see parts of it had been destroyed by fire. Open doors in her field of vision suggested the place had more than one purpose.

Approaching the nearest entrance, she double-checked the readiness of her pistol. The bulky load on her back scraped against the doorframe when she stepped into the gutted interior.

Unexpected trash littered the floor under her slow-moving feet. She found herself looking at a wide variety of food wrappers. The sight of so much pre-

Collapse garbage made her think of the two remaining, very old, freeze-dried meals she still had in her pack. "Nobody has this much food. Looks like a lot of somebodies have deliberately dropped their trash here for a long time."

Acting on a hunch, Dar went back outside to look for the power cord attached to the base of the pedestal. She followed it cautiously with her flashlight into a dark doorway that was not quite so cluttered. The beam illuminated the interior of a very small room, just big enough for her to stand in and close the door behind her—if there had been one.

She studied the far wall of the little room for several seconds, slowly realizing it was actually a solid metal door. "Okay, I'll bite. Small room with a door flush to the wall. Floor to ceiling, wall to wall."

Dar turned off the beam of her flashlight. She waited patiently for her eyes to adjust to the darkness.

A small indicator light on the grimy wall next to the formidable metal door was easy to miss. It glowed green. She probed with the fingers of her free hand to find and grasp the strange compass. As if on cue, the face of the gadget showed its green dot.

Nocturnal noises made her feel exposed, Dar was almost ready to hate the gadget—again—when the symbol began to blink on and off.

"Could be dirty," she decided. Fogging the display with her breath, she rubbed it on her shirt. She was rewarded with a grinding sound from the metal door. The tiny light next to it flickered on and off as the door noisily slid open.

Dar activated her flashlight and raised her pistol before the door stopped moving. Her light revealed a larger interior area that was partially obscured by curtains of dusty cobwebs. She took a moment to notice the rusty, gritty, narrow track the door slid open on. "Somebody has been banging on you very hard," she concluded.

Dar hesitated when she remembered something the merchant Marsh had said many times about locked doors. "Pre-Collapse people locked their doors for a reason," she recalled. "To keep something safe or to hide from something dangerous."

She reminisced fleetingly about the fascination her brother Jack used to have with horror stories told so graphically by elderly family members and ghoulish neighbors. Those exaggerations were always so gory, she'd never been able to take them seriously. Alone, in the dark, deep inside an abandoned relocation camp with no one to help her, she paused in an effort to will away her fears.

Summoning her grit, Dar adjusted her glasses and secured the flashlight on her vest. Gripping her loaded semiautomatic pistol with one hand, she stepped in to the unknown.

* * *

Dar had seen color images of pre-Collapse white collar offices in books, magazines, and movies. She knew she was walking into what had been ridiculed as a 'cubicle farm.' The maze of bland modular furniture, made into small workspaces for dozens, or hundreds, of busy people, was just as quiet as it was murky. She walked at left or right angles to let the flashlight clipped to her vest roam over dust-covered phones, computers, and chairs.

She refused to look downward at whatever was crunching under her shuffling feet. "It's not human bones," she told herself. "There are no dead people in here. It's just me. I'm not walking on bones. I would never do that."

Dar froze when a computer screen on a desk in the cubicle in front of her powered up. Gray-white static filled the display, slowly replaced by an abstract test pattern image with bold text: Please Stand By. Recognizing it was instinctively unsettling. Despite the unrelenting passage of time, common knowledge still enshrined the meaning of that pattern and those words.

"That's not funny!" she protested loudly to whoever might be listening.

A single overhead light came on, casting a circle of light around the cobweb-covered chair in the cubicle. Dar looked skeptically at the ceiling, then down at the chair. The gadget in her pocket beeped again. She slapped the pocket it was in. "Be quiet, you!"

The noisy beeping continued, making her feel more uncomfortable than she had been. Knowing what computers were didn't help. Every dust-covered object that she could see was just too macabre. The gun in her hand felt inadequate.

"Is anyone else in here?"

She cleared her throat while slowly turning in place. Debris crunched under her feet. "Come on out!" she shouted.

Her voice echoed off the high, gloomy ceiling. The small, round, overhead light fixture put out just enough illumination to highlight the abandoned chair without spilling over into other nearby workstations.

She ignored the beeping in her vest pocket, deliberately pointing her pistol at the flat screen. "Tell me something right now, or I'm going to stop standing by!"

Letters formed on the screen: You Are Not Supposed to Be Here.

"No kidding!" she scoffed. "It's not my fault. I have a lousy compass."

It's Not A Compass, the screen spelled.

Dar used her free hand to rip open her vest pocket and pull out the beeping gadget. "Turn it off or I'm going to start shooting!"

The gadget in her hand stopped beeping. "Okay, that's a start. What is this thing?"

The display revealed: It's A Location Finder.

The fearful teen's skin crawled as she put the silent object back in her vest pocket. She turned off her flashlight. "Yeah, well. This is a location. I'm here. Didn't need this dumb thing to get here, either! Found it all by myself."

Lucky, the monitor replied.

"Says you," she snorted. "Look. Just tell me. Is this Haven? I was hoping for more. If this is all of it, I mean—"

The screen shimmered: No.

As her eyes fully adjusted to the overhead light, Dar found it harder to see other parts of the large room she was in. Unfamiliar surfaces here and there reflected small amounts of soft light without revealing what those things were.

"I haven't been sleeping very much," she reasoned to herself. "Not much to eat or drink. The last good meal I had was a bunch of greasy hot dogs. I might just be sick and this is only a bad dream. If this isn't Haven, where is it?"

Letters and numbers flashed across the screen before it read: What Is Haven to You?

Dar's disappointment got the best of her. She slumped.

"Right now, it's a stupid idea and I was foolish for thinking it was real. I don't care if it was or is more than one place. Look," she sniffled. "I've got some really bad people after me. They attacked our home, killed my whole family. All I want to do right now is get to some place safe, you know?"

She made her gun safe while gathering her wits.

"I found out just a few days ago, my grandfather had something to do with Haven. He was there, he went there, or something.

"All that trouble following me. Nothing slows them down. They don't seem to care who they hurt. I was hoping I could go somewhere else that was away from the school. Maybe take the danger away from them, if I could."

Letters on the screen changed to read: Lambert, Henry C.

"That's him."

The grimy monitor's visual field filled with bright green text: Use The Locator. Follow The Arrow. Stay Alive.

Dar flinched. "Ha! That's easy for you to say. You don't have to go back out there. Sorel Taggert is somewhere between me and the school. His older brother, Ben, is dead. There was no other way. I had to. I— he— Ben killed a friend of mine. She was a cop.

"That one-eyed man is evil enough for three people. Really. I saw Helen face him down. He won't stop looking for me, until, you know, I'm dead."

The displayed green text flashed: Use The Locator. Follow The Arrow. Stay Alive.

Dar defensively reached for the shotgun that rode on her pack. She hesitated, digging the gadget out of her pocket. Cupping it in her hand, she pressed the seek button with one finger. The now-familiar digitally displayed arrow swung slowly to the northwest.

"I must be crazy for talking to a machine. Things like you don't have a good track record with people."

Red lines on the screen formed a frowning face.

"I don't want to hear it!" she fumed. "My parents always told me: do the right thing. Over and over again; do the right thing! Then, along come those

Taggert bastards. Who do they think they are? Somebody needs to stop them."

Dar held up the gadget with one hand while wiping stray hairs from her smudged face. She looked meaningfully at the screen. "How do I know this thing really could help me find a safe place? What if all it leads me to is more dead stuff like this?"

Sparkles flew across the screen. The red frown was replaced by vibrant text that read: Go At Sunrise. Make Your Future.

Dar wiped her nose as the screen went blank. Gripped by a wave of cold insecurity, she looked up and down the aisle she was in. Then, she glance up at the overhead light. "Hey! Where can I get a drink of water? Some place to sleep without being attacked would be nice. I've come this far with all my fingers and toes. Might be fun to make it the rest of the way in one piece, if I can."

The overhead light winked out, leaving her in total darkness.

CHAPTER FOURTEEN

Dar turned on the flashlight clipped to her vest. She moved slowly to reach for the grip of the short-barreled pump shotgun that hung on her rucksack. Pleased with herself for making very little noise, she held the gun in both hands for several seconds before cocking it with one fast, fluid motion. The old scattergun let out a double metallic click that sounded louder than it really was.

Remembering what she'd been taught by her parents, Dar took two steps and paused to look around before she moved again. What had once been a game played in the confines of their warm farmhouse on a cold winter's day was now becoming real skill.

At the end of the aisle, she could see a short, wide hallway that was strewn with more of the same trash she'd been walking through. The rusting wreck of a military police robot blocked her view of whatever might be at the end of the corridor.

Dar turned in her tracks, straining to hear the smallest sound. "This would be the part where Jack comes out of nowhere to laugh while he's blasting paintballs into my back. Not today big brother. Not today."

Joking about her brother made Dar think about the way he so morbidly enjoyed the stories older people told about murderous machines. Remembering his fascination caused her to remember bits and pieces of what she'd read in Helen's borrowed books.

"No. Wait. Military police were good guys. That's you, right? Now, you're out here all by yourself."

She put her light on the MP bot's rusting frame. "You must've been scary in your day."

Dar looked it up and down, taking note of its broad shoulders, large, cleated feet, and what might have been olive drab skin.

"Paint," she reminded herself. "You were painted. Not quite like our house, but you get the idea. Looks like you weren't as bullet-resistant as the bathroom I found in that charging station."

The bot remained motionless. Optical sensors on its cranium pivoted left and right.

Startled, Dar pointed her shotgun at the machine's torso. "Are you still in there?" She took a step closer. "Come on, do it again!"

The mechanical eyes on the stationary robot moved back and forth.

"Once more." Dar's jaw dropped open when she saw both eyes move. "Let me guess. You're here keeping an eye on the place?"

The bot didn't respond.

Dar laughed. "Don't take it personally. I'm having my own bad day. I know a merchant who would give half of what he owns just for a look at you. Makes me wish you could talk. Is there anything else you can do?"

The robot raised its right arm, which contained a rotary gun system. The mechanism whirled to life, then fell silent.

Dar watched the gun barrels slow and stop. "What's that? A shotgun?"

The MP unit's eyes rotated rapidly. Dar snickered. "I'll take that as 'yes.'"

She bent over to see past the robot. "That's a short hallway," she decided. "Looks like just a few rooms. Just what fugitives like me need for a few hours of sleep."

Dar walked around the immobilized robot, into the confined space. Her light found two doors: one to the left, the other to the right, which was open.

Leading with her shotgun, she peered in without filling the doorway. In the sweep of her beam, she saw blankets and bedrolls piled in separate corners. Pairs of dirty boots and shoes were lined up along one wall. A mound of dirty, once-colorful clothes filled the center of the floor. Everything stank with the odor of unwashed bodies.

Dar backed away from the reek. "Did you know this was in here?" she asked the bot.

She shook her head. A second glance allowed her to understand what she was seeing. The room had been used by many travelers, over the years, to rest or resupply. She looked down at her own muddy pant legs and boots.

Dar imagined dozens of men and women coming and going over the years. She put herself in their place, realizing that she might follow their example and leave something behind for the next person who might need it.

Turning her light on the door across the hall, she was able to nudge it open with the barrel of her shotgun. Dar grumbled to let off steam. "Sure. Make yourself at home. Come right on in. Nobody here but half-dead robots and people running for their lives. Sit down, rest awhile. What could go wrong?"

She was startled to see the answer to her question when the beam of her flashlight revealed a trio of human skulls and the same number of broken helmets scattered on the floor in front of her. The room was larger than she'd expected. That revelation was enough to make her reexamine the grisly debris on the floor. Squinting attentively in the low light, she guessed that all three antiballistic helmets had been shot to pieces—while their owners were still wearing them.

Dar tried to calm herself. "I know what messy rooms are, especially my bedroom. These things didn't fall where they are. Somebody put them here to make me see them."

She paused. "So. Let's think. Anyone who comes in here would see it, or step on it. I'm here. I'm creeped out, and—I step over the dead stuff."

Something didn't feel right. Dar stood up straight to let her light brighten the room.

Empty chairs in front of consoles indicated where most of the workstations were located. From her vantage point, she could see what looked like telephones and headsets on some consoles crammed in next to unfamiliar devices. On the far side of the dim room, she saw a wide variety of hats and coats labeled with emergency service logos.

She made another pass around the room with her flashlight, realizing that there were no bullet holes in the walls or on the ceiling. None of the electronics appeared damaged. "Can't see any signs of fire. Whatever killed you guys didn't happen here in this room. So, why are you here?"

Dar got down on one knee to point her small light at each skull and piece of helmet. Scattered light reflected off a thin, transparent string that seemed to be hanging in mid-air.

"Tripwire," she breathed.

Dar squirmed from side to side, wriggling backward, away from the unobvious threat. She stood up without caring what crunched under her feet. She was unable to see what the string was connected to, only that it was just high enough to snag on her boot when she moved. "Yikes! Step without looking and paint the wall!"

"I'm not ready for this," she decided, continuing to back away from the door. Whatever was in that room might not be worth the risk of getting hurt.

Dar used the beam of her flashlight to thoroughly examine the EMS garb that was hanging on the wall. She recognized some of the hats and coats as police and fire gear. She lingered over a single blue jacket with big yellow letters on it. "F-B-I," she spelled, "Whatever that is, or was."

Dar looked down at the floor to be sure she was stepping away from the room with as much caution as she was capable of. Tarnished bullet casings rolled under her feet. She kicked them away.

She prowled out of the short hallway, around the immobilized robot, parallel to the cubicle farm. Her wavering flashlight revealed a rubble-strewn stairwell that she ignored. A single room with a dented door contained two rusting bunk beds with smelly mattresses. Bullet holes perforated every wall and the ceiling.

"Somebody didn't sleep well," she snorted.

Dar pulled off her load. "Beggars can't be choosers," she reminded herself, dropping the rucksacks on the floor.

The shotgun in her hand began to feel heavy. She sat on one of the lower bunks and laid the gun aside on the squeaking mattress. Standing slowly, she walked over to inspect the door. Her flashlight beam fell on a crude cast iron deadbolt that she could lock from inside the room. She leaned over to see it more clearly. "Will you look at that?"

Dar went back to sit next to her shotgun. She rummaged in her vest pocket for the locator gadget. Holding it in her right hand, she ate some beef jerky with her left hand. "So. People use this thing, or something like it, to come here. Once they get this far, they obviously don't stay very long. Why? They're on their way to somewhere else. Coming or going, they stop here for a rest. Okay, I'll buy that. I am going toward Haven, to the place. That means somebody who is already there comes here. Where in the world would they be going to from here?"

The riddle was more than a tired, hungry teenager could handle on an empty stomach. Laying down, Dar turned off her flashlight and napped restlessly. Every squeak of the mattress or bunk frame brought her back from the edge of relaxing sleep.

She awakened, hours later, in a bad mood. Disoriented by the unfamiliar feel of the place, she fumbled around in the darkness for her things. Shouldering both rucksacks, she held her shotgun at the ready before releasing the deadbolt to open the door of the bunkroom.

Hungry and dehydrated, she paused in front of the immobilized robot, turning on the flashlight that was still clipped to her vest. "No offense, but I hope you never see me again."

She cleaned her glasses with a handkerchief before retracing her steps to find a way out of the tomb-like interior of the structure.

In the shambles of what had been somebody's office, she slipped out through a jagged hole in the wall, into early morning daylight. A quick look at her watch indicated it was just after 6 a.m. "Getting lazy," she muttered. "Startin' to sleep late. Bad habit."

Dar's mood improved after she'd been walking for an hour. The last of Ben Taggert's beef jerky and one of the remaining candy bars silenced her stomach. She swigged from her water bottle sparingly as the eastward rise of the sun became more apparent through the trees.

A quick check of the locator in her pocket was not as reassuring as she'd hoped it would be. Unanswered questions bounced around in her mind while she moved west. The unmistakable smell of burning wood brought her back to reality.

* * *

Dar remembered Bellamy's warning to stay away from any of the few homesteads she might encounter while making her way toward Delphi. Despite the rail line that ran through the forest between Belmore and Delphi, very little was known about who or what might still be in there. Anyone who chose to live in such seclusion might go unnoticed for years, or even decades.

That possibility was neither strange nor unusual to Dar. Her own industrious family had come to rely on the unique freedoms and opportunities that remoteness provided for anyone who preferred to be self-sufficient. The fact that it would take her two hours or more to reach many of her favorite neighbors on foot was considered to be a good thing.

Dar thought about that attitude and the reflex to be cautious it often inspired in her. She sniffed the air for any hint of manure. She'd be too close if she could smell it.

Closing her eyes, Dar picked out the scents of wood smoke, evergreen needles, and compost. From experience, she knew they were persistent odors that could waft over long distances on the slightest breeze.

She softly backtracked over open ground until the aroma of wood smoke diminished. Seeing no sign of the ruined road, she consulted the locator while observing the overhead path of the sun.

Tense minutes became nerve-racking hours. She made her way through one copse of trees after another. Seeing a handmade rabbit snare hanging low in a bush, she turned out and away from it, veering east in an effort to avoid detection.

Dar stopped at midday to rest and refresh herself near a small creek. Feeling relieved, she refilled her water bottle. Adding water to a freeze-dried meal, she tried to eat without reading what was on the label.

After a few chewy bites, instinct and curiosity took over. "'Contains no animal protein, real or synthetic. Fabricated from 50% Nutriplex and 50% Phytoscine.' Yuck, this tastes like grass! '1 serving per container. Simulated vegetable nutriment suitable for humans. Ideal for low carb and vegetarian lifestyles.' I doubt that very much."

When she was finished eating the unpleasant food, Dar used the folding shovel to dig a hole and hide her accumulated trash. She was kicking dead leaves over the packed earth when she heard the train from Belmore passing in the distance. Sounds of clattering metal and creaking wood got closer. She flinched when the clanking locomotive's air horns blared to signal a stop. "Somebody is getting on or they're getting off."

Dar put away her shovel. She jogged away from the sound of the noisy, idling train, hoping to get far away from it before anyone saw her.

Reinvigorated by food and water, she loped at a steady pace, darting between trees and dashing through clearings as fast as she could go without being winded. Scampering through a dense thicket, she ran into a roadside guardrail that was hidden by tall grass. Flipping head over heels, she felt the rucksacks slide off and fly away before she landed flat on her back in the brush. The impact jarred her glasses off her face.

Dar clutched the shotgun in her aching arms while gasping for air. She took a breath and held it to avoid any further panic. She exhaled with a phlegmy cough as the sound of barking dogs reached her ears.

Within seconds, she was certain they were coming closer. She rolled over to search for her glasses. Putting the shotgun aside, she patted the ground with both hands. "Come on, come on! Don't do this to me!"

Some part of her began to understand that she was hearing the approach of two dogs, not four or more. That knowledge didn't make her any less nervous; it only underscored the fact that she was in trouble. Shooting them was not unthinkable. She'd done it before, on the family farm, when feral strays threatened their chickens, pigs, and Gerry the cow.

Thrashing through thorns and weeds as fast as she could, her cut and bleeding hands probed for the missing glasses. The barking of the dogs was punctuated by the sound of shouting voices.

"Two dogs and two people," she decided while crawling clumsily over a rotten log. "That's just great!"

The thin branches of a bush slapped her in the face just as her fingers found her glasses. She spit out broken leaves and swore while getting to her feet. Dar was reaching for her shotgun when one of the tracking dogs bounded soundlessly out of the brush behind her. She turned as it ran toward her with snarling jaws wide open. The rushing animal was blurry, though discernable. Holding her glasses in one hand, she raised the shotgun with the other and pulled the trigger.

Wildlife bolted and birds flew when the scattergun boomed. The attacking dog fell with a shriek and lay motionless.

Dar ignored warm flecks that settled on her face and hands. She put her glasses on and ran for the rucksacks, which lay nearby. Snatching them up, she fled over open ground as fast as she could go.

Bearing the load, she efficiently pumped a shell into the breech of the shotgun. Rifle shots echoed behind her as she ran. "Bad guess!" she snorted.

Dar slowed and stopped when she saw what looked like a portion of the old roadbed she had walked on a day earlier. She looked over her shoulder.

"Something tells me you guys know this area better than I do. You'd be expecting me to use all the open ground I can find to get away. So." She paused to squint thoughtfully at the forest surrounding her. "You've got one dog. You'll use it to follow my scent.

Even if you don't live around here, you can still figure out which way I'm going. If you do live in these woods, you'll know where I'm going and get there ahead of me."

The departure of the train was signaled by a blast from its three distinctive air horns. Dar thought about the direction that sound came from. Inspiration blossomed in her mind as she wiped gore off her glasses.

When she was a little girl, the stories she heard about humans being hunted by machines were just too terrible. They kept her awake at night. Something her father had said caused her to recall with a smile how much Jack enjoyed all of it.

"Man or machine," she remembered, "they all hunt the same way. Always looking for any sign of what you did. Do what they don't expect and you're bound to get away."

Dar took a few uncertain steps and stopped. "What are you expecting?"

The problem was aggravating. She popped a piece of chewing gum into her mouth. Chomping while she walked, Dar's gaze went from the roadbed to the direction of the fading sound of the rolling train.

When she looked at it with one hand, the arrow on the locator swung resolutely west. Indecisive, Dar put the gadget away and walked until she heard the bark and bay of a single dog closing in from behind her.

The roadbed was visible, turning slowly westward through a thinning expanse of sparse trees. She was surprised to see that it intersected the train track at a manmade rail crossing.

Dar trotted onto the track and stopped. Early afternoon sun glinted off the southernmost surface of Black Lake. "One mile, maybe two," she decided.

Remembering that Bellamy had warned her to stay away from the train and its tracks, Dar hurried into the trees on the far side of the line, into what she hoped would be safer terrain that would block her from casual view.

Rubbing crusted blood off her aching fingers, she wiped sweaty palms on her dirty pants. Twice in the span of an hour, she heard the bark of the canine that was tracking her. It got closer, then faded away. Outpacing the animal didn't make her feel better.

"Smarter than a dog, but not by much."

Dar thought about veering toward the lake. As enticing as the thought of more water was, she decided against it.

"Must be a lot of homesteads right on the lake. Not quite so many inland, away from the water. Only time they might cross paths with each other is when they hear the train coming or going."

She walked calmly back out onto the rusting track. Gravel crunched under her feet.

"East is Belmore." She pointed in the direction she'd come from. "West is about that way. If I was a train, everyone with good ears could hear me coming. I am not a train; anyone who does not hear me has to see me or I pass right on by."

Dar alternated between a fast walk and a slow jog, making her way west on the track bed for more than a full hour.

Late afternoon sun fell directly upon her as she slowed to approach a gradual turn. Broken chain link fencing on the lakeward side of the track was visible through bushes and weeds. A faded sign declared: Evergreen Beach Club, Private Property. A smaller, handmade, wooden sign erected near the tracks would be visible to passengers on the train. Its painted letters simply said: Delphi, 5 miles.

Her back ached enough to make Dar groan. Victory over the tracking dogs seemed unimportant as she looked for any sign of continued pursuit.

"I really wouldn't want them to follow me, that's for sure!"

The recognizable smell of cook fires and the time displayed on her wristwatch told Dar that area residents were starting to make dinner. Boiling soups or baking breads were well known for making smells that could drift a long way. That olfactory clue was also a danger sign. She was closer than she should be to fiercely independent people who didn't know her.

"Put the gun away," she admonished herself. "I'm just another kid you see every day walking on the tracks. For all you know, I'm just going to the neighbor's place."

Slinging the shotgun allowed her arms to rest. She slowed down, ambling as casually as she could pretend. The track crested a hill before descending into a shallow valley.

What had been a golf course was now irrigated farmland that sloped down to the gravelly south shore of Black Lake.

Dar marveled, "Wow! Glad I don't have to harvest that!"

Enclave walls were clearly visible from where she stood. Here and there, parts of paved roads were still in use, connected by cobblestone or gravel paths. The protected portion of the community was hard to judge at such a great distance. It appeared to be similar in size to Belmore, though she couldn't be sure.

Dar took the locator out of her vest pocket. "Tell me something," she asked wearily while pushing the seek button.

The arrow indicated northwest. Dar's heart sank when she looked in that direction. In the far distance, bathed in golden afternoon light, she saw a verdant green mountain, studded with trees, dominate the horizon.

"No…" she pled weakly, "I'm so very tired."

CHAPTER FIFTEEN

From the large, second-story window of a post-Collapse home that belonged to a friend, Sorel Taggert used a pair of borrowed binoculars to extend his vision. He considered his options while observing the railroad tracks and farmland that were within his visual field. Two out of three search teams with dogs he'd sent into the forest by train to search for the girl were back with no news.

"Might not mean anything," he told his host while using his one good eye to go over the land one more time. "Tracking dogs have minds of their own. For all we know, they got themselves lost. From what I've seen of her, Darlene Lambert isn't a match for them. It'll be dumb luck if she gets here."

Sorel prided himself on being aware of things that most people could easily overlook. No detail was too small for his attention, not even when he was enjoying the comforts of clean clothes and a bed without bugs

His freshly laundered, brown static camouflage shirt and pants were crisp and his worn boots were spotless. Washed and combed hair made his black eyepatch stand out just a little more.

Behind him, his host waited patiently. Dressed in clean pre-Collapse casual wear with matching shoes, Marcus Partridge was only slightly annoyed by the use of his home. He was related to the Taggerts by marriage, a fact that, until now had always come with very few strings.

"Don't worry about it," he reassured while pacing around the confines of his lavishly furnished study.

"My contacts are solid. Dead or alive, they'll tell me if, or when, she turns up."

Sorel lowered the binoculars, he put them on a nearby table before turning to Marcus. "Have you ever met Seth?"

"No."

The one-eyed man blinked. "He's not our father. Trust me on that. He never has had much tolerance for mistakes—or loose ends. Know what I mean? I think they used to call people like him overachievers. For as long as I can remember, nothing is good enough for him. Always room for improvement, blah-blah-blah."

Marcus came to a stop near his favorite bookshelf. "Yes, I do know the type. You might want to think about coming out here. Could be more opportunities for somebody who can get things done, even if they aren't always perfect."

"Our influence will reach out this far soon enough," Sorel said matter-of-factly, "Getting a grip on the farms around Tumwater makes that much clear to me. Now that they are gone, the Lamberts and all the others like them won't make any more trouble. When word gets out that we solved this problem, people around here will begin to see that we are the law. That'll be a step in the right direction."

Marcus was a career politician with future ambitions of being the mayor of Delphi. He kept his thoughts to himself. The inhabitants of his enclave had one thing in common with their neighbors in Belmore. They had no taste for Taggert justice. No matter how many pre-Collapse Federal government directives they still claimed to enforce, there was no statute language in any of them that conferred the hereditary leadership claimed by the Taggert clan through their extended family.

"She's just one—"

Sorel focused his fury on Marcus. "Only takes one malcontent to spread a bad idea. I'd bet you everything I own, what's-her-name is out there now, trying to find a way to get to that school! Do you really think she's just going to forget about what has happened over the last four or five lousy days? I wouldn't, and neither would you. As long as she lives, she's going to be talking to somebody about her issues, grievances, or whatever the folks out here like to call it!"

Marcus fidgeted with one of the old keepsakes on a shelf without looking at Sorel. "The absence of law leads to chaos. 'Order' is often a matter of semantics. I just want you to make it clear to the rest of the family that I and my household have cooperated completely. When your influence does reach out this far, I want—"

"I'll tell 'em," Sorel snapped.

Marcus reined himself in. "You've got your bases covered. Why don't we go down for some drinks before dinner?"

Sorel looked around the opulent room. "Ben hasn't turned up yet."

The politician shrugged. "We were both there when the train pulled in. You heard what the passengers said. No reason to think they'd lie about something that extreme. She jumped and he went after her."

"That's why I sent the dog teams!" Sorel replied peevishly. "Ben is a big fella with even bigger feet. A blind man could find that clumsy ox in a snowstorm! Just doesn't feel right. How could four good sniffers not run into him?"

Marcus tried to be reassuring. "It's not your problem."

Sorel pivoted. "No. Everyone who saw it, including both of the train conductors, said the cop shot Zeke when they forced their way in. Three shots. That's professional."

"What are you saying?"

"I just don't know," Sorel pondered pessimistically. "Either that cop is very dead or Ben is. He's not a woodsman. I have always been a better tracker than he wanted to be. He never learned the basics when he had the chance. Used to make our father so angry. He'd say we deserved to die, face down in the dirt, because we didn't pay attention."

The older man stepped toward the door. "You're putting a lot on somebody who isn't here right now. Give him a chance to finish what he started. Really, there's nothing else for you to do."

Sorel followed Marcus into the hallway. "Actually, there is. Go ahead. Get dinner. Don't wait for me. I'm going out with as many of our men as I can round up in a hurry. If anyone asks, tell them I want to see what happens outside the enclave walls after dark. What time do they close the gates?"

"Nine p.m.," Marcus remembered. "You really think she would just walk right in?"

Sorel followed Marcus down the stairs to the ground floor. "Why wouldn't she?"

* * *

Dar rested in the tree line while the setting sun blanketed the enclave in cool shadows that would hide her from casual view at a distance. Slowly nibbling her last candy bar, she watched people come and go. Some of them guided livestock on paths. Others made their way purposefully through rows of high wheat. As the hours passed, wranglers and field hands became fewer and fewer.

She started walking down the shoulder of the train track, toward the nearest dirt road, when she thought most people would be busy with end of the day chores or even dinner. She stuffed the shotgun deep into the folds of her bundled rucksacks so it wouldn't be obvious that she was armed.

Dar measured her pace as she got closer to the enclave. "Just another person on their way home from doing something, whatever it is you guys do around here."

Most of what she saw reminded her of the rolling countryside around her family farm. The digital arrow on the irritating, impersonal locator pointed north when she looked at it, right at the looming expanse of Capitol Peak. Strolling downhill on a well-used dirt track was calming enough to make her feel better about being so much closer to the school.

"Must be inside the walls of the enclave," she decided when she came to a crossroad, "Can't imagine they'd put something that important out here."

Thinking about the school, and the safety it represented, made Dar stop in her tracks. She was close enough to the scattered structures outside the earthen walls of the enclave to see rooftops and chimneys.

"What am I doing?" she worried.

The brazen words of Ben Taggert came back to her. Shortly before he died, he said something about his brother Sorel—the one-eyed man—who was already waiting for her.

"He got here ahead of me," she mumbled.

Fear became frustration before her willpower transformed it into a sense of purpose. She didn't want to bring her predicament into the school, where teachers and students might be harmed. As grief-stricken and angry as she had been, Dar was determined to do something, anything, that would slow or stop the Taggerts' aggression.

Her nose detected the familiar mouth-watering aroma of grilled hot dogs sizzling on a grill nearby. Enticed by the smell, she began looking through her pockets for loose scrip while she walked. Dar got close enough to the south gate of the enclave to see it—a large, hand-painted sign declared what the local scrip was and rates of exchange for other forms of money, including gold.

She stood in a short, fast line at a busy vendor shack. "Two please," she ordered when it was her turn.

Dar tried to stand out of the way, away from suspicious, prying eyes. She ate hungrily.

Before she could finish her first hot dog, she was noisily surrounded by a chatty crowd who seemed to know each other quite well.

Dar relaxed while she ate. She was surprised by how refreshing it felt to be near people who didn't want to harm her.

Dar was so caught up in the life-affirming moment, she didn't noticed the young man who was trying to stand next to her. She bumped into him while powering through her second hot dog.

"Excuse me," he apologized.

She cursed herself for being so unobservant. The setting sun was below the horizon. Darkness would be on them in a matter of minutes and she'd been caught daydreaming!

Dar turned to face him defiantly, "Hey! Watch where you're going. I'm standing here."

The handsome teenager grinned at her, holding a paper cone of french fries in his hands. "Sorry. We all just got out of school and it's the weekend."

"What?"

"Weekend," he repeated while being jostled. "No school on the weekend, you know? A break from the drudge. Time to catch up on sleep and maybe get some homework done. Any of that sound familiar?"

Dar was still off balance. "Friday. That means today is Friday! Yes, well. Of course. School schedule, five days a week. Right."

He offered her his right hand. “Hi, my name is Evan. I haven’t seen you here before. You must be new.”

She shook his warm, greasy hand with her own mustard-stained fingers. “Yes, new.”

People around them continued to chat loudly.

Evan ate while he talked. “Thought so. It’s that time of year. New students are coming in from all over the place.”

Dar didn’t know what else to say for several seconds. Many of the people around her wore clean clothes; Evan himself was dressed casually. She finished off her last hot dog.

“Do I look like a student?”

Evan gave her an appraising look. “You are…not dirty enough to be a field hand.”

Dar laughed when she looked down at her blood-spattered clothing and muddy boots. “You guys make this kind of mess in a classroom?”

“Sometimes,” Evan admitted between mouthfuls. “Depends on what class you’re in. They teach livestock here—feeding, breeding, and butchering.”

“Sounds like you’ve done it,” she surmised from his tone of voice.

He shrugged while finishing his food. “I learned the basics to make my folks happy. Now, I can’t eat hot dogs because I know what’s in them!”

“Trust me,” Dar insisted sarcastically while wiping her hands on the legs of her pants. “I grew up on a farm, and I made sausage!”

Evan crumpled the empty cone in his hand. “That is brave. Do you mind if I ask, what’s your name?”

Dar’s pulse began to race. The question was fair. Answering it would mean an end to her anonymity. “I— Well— Look, I wasn’t supposed to be here for another month at least. They might not be expecting me quite so soon. I don't want to get anyone in trouble because I showed up early."

Evan could see how uneasy she was. "You've got your letter, don't you? That's all you need to get in. Your family takes care of the payment."

She took a deep breath. Evan was easy to talk with. It was hard to resist the urge to unburden herself.

"That's not it. I've got a different kind of problem; it's following me."

"Taggerts," Evan guessed.

Dar was amazed. "How did you know?"

He shrugged as somebody bumped in to him. "It's not a secret. Everybody knows. They have Tumwater in their pocket. It's okay, though; their influence doesn't quite reach out this far. How much of a problem have they been for you?"

"Some."

"Yeah," he nodded. "They can be hard to avoid when they are in town."

She cringed. "Are any of them here now?"

Evan frowned. "Yeah. Now that you mention it, Sorel Taggert is prowling around. That one-eyed menace is hard to miss."

"What do you know about him," Dar asked, dreading the answer.

Sensing her growing fear, Evan looked over his should. "Only what the gossip says. Bloodthirsty killer, that sort of thing. Let me talk to my friends for a minute. I'll see if they know any more."

Dar's stomach lurched, she watched Evan turn and plunge into the boisterous crowd.

He returned minutes later with bad news. "Sorel Taggert is out and about with hired guns near the south gate. From what I've just been told, he got there about five minutes ago. We probably walked right past him on our way out here. Sorry, I didn't know—"

With non-threatening people to shield her from casual view, Dar was able to think. "It's okay. I've already figured out that I can't stay here, not without bringing—you know, *that*—in close enough to get somebody hurt. I'll go around him."

Evan liked her sensibility. "Delphi is like a lot of places. They've got north, south, east, and west gates in the earthworks. I'll bet you two more hot dogs that Taggert has all of them staked out."

Dar was glum. "Probably."

Evan smirked with inspiration. "I'll be 17 in three months. You can't be any older than I am. You fit right in. Why don't you just walk back inside with the rest of us? He won't dare try anything so close to the gate sentries. They'd shoot him full of holes if he did. You'd be safe, once you're inside."

Dar thought about the locator gadget in her vest pocket. As tempting as Haven was, the school and everything it promised was closer. If the police in Delphi were anything like their counterparts in Belmore, she would, however reluctantly, be welcomed as a paying student. The notion of being surrounded by so many people who didn't care for the Taggerts and their way of doing thing was inviting. If there was any truth to be found about Haven, it would just have to wait.

"It's worth a try," she decided.

Within minutes, Dar was surrounded by a raucous crowd of teenagers. Some of them peppered her with questions. She answered very few.

"Come on guys," Evan protested by her side, "Leave her alone. Everyone, just remember to play it cool when we get to the gate. Taggert and his bullies aren't allowed inside the enclave. Once we're in behind those walls, everything will be fine."

Dar tried to make some small talk while they walked. "What do you guys hear about Haven around here?"

Some in the crowd laughed. Others answered briefly with what little they'd heard from strangers who were passing through.

Evan was more forthcoming. "A lot of us have thought about trying to put the pieces together. I suppose that's why so many people spend years at a time in the ruins. Is that what you want do to, eventually? Go looking for whatever Haven really is?"

Dar thought about the locator in her vest pocket. "I once met somebody who had a large collection of things related to Haven. They had it all spread out over the walls of a room. Newspapers, magazines, some handwritten stuff."

Evan was impressed. "What was it like? Did you learn anything?"

Dar shrugged as they turned a corner. "It's hard to explain. Standing right there in the middle of it all, I was tempted."

"What was that like?"

She snickered. "I've heard stories about people who get gold fever. They run off in to the hills and they won't stop digging."

Evan pointed at the south gate when it came into view. "I've heard scavengers are like that, especially the ones who come back with good loot. I've seen a few of the things they pass around here. It's pretty wild stuff. When I think about what this community could do with things like that, I'm almost willing. Almost, but not quite."

"What stops you?" Dar asked.

He scowled. "Better proof. Something, anything, that's directly connected to Haven. Who am I kidding? Anyone who actually had that would certainly keep it to themselves. Slow down, we're almost to the gate. Keep your head down and don't stop. Just walk!"

CHAPTER SIXTEEN

Sorel Taggert stood in the glare of the streetlights mounted high on the earthen walls near the south gate to Delphi.

The enclave's defenders had turned out, in force, to block his entry in to the fortified town. Men and women, wearing scarred body armor, watched what he and his armed posse did from the safety of their barricades. As long as they stayed outside the walls without shooting anyone, the Taggerts could do as they pleased.

The presence of a 20-millimeter cannon on a sandbagged turret over the gate was more than enough to make Sorel feel uncomfortable. He didn't like having his back to that much firepower. The brazen gesture was necessary to reinforce the perception that he was in command of the situation.

Sorel knew he was gambling. With four hired guns watching four entrances, he risked allowing Dar to slip right on by without his crew of shotgun-wielding brawlers noticing.

"This is the closest entrance to the school," he told his henchmen confidently. "Shortest line between two points and all that. Everyone knows what their job is."

They did. Dressed in rugged, outdoor work clothes, they looked much like the people who lived and worked in the surrounding area. Their assorted shotguns were loaded with a mixture of nonlethal ammunition types. As long as they didn't draw blood or kill, the enclave's defenders would stay behind their wall and out of the way.

From past, grim experience, Sorel knew how it would go down, if it happened at all. Everything he knew about the Lambert family suggested they were typical homesteaders. Their sense of right and wrong was often encouraged by what made them self-sufficient. Dar might not come here if she thought her presence would bring trouble to the enclave.

Sorel heard the sound of approaching voices. He checked his watch. "Been dark for almost a full hour. Keep your eyes open! Everyone who comes this way wants to go in before they shut the gates. Pay attention to what you see. Fear of being locked out for the night is not the same as what they feel about you!"

All four men laughed. Two of them swore. Being disliked when far away from Tumwater was just a part of their job.

Sorel hitched up his gun belt when he saw a large crowd approaching. "Pay attention!" he warned the ruffians behind him. "Keep your eyes open. Look for anyone who is not looking right at you. Remember what I told you. There's a big difference between hatred, curiosity, and fear."

* * *

Dar became more alert when she got her first glimpse of Sorel. Brown camouflage made him and his goons stand out in the harsh bright light emanating from the fortified gate. Her apprehension faded as each step brought her closer to the man who had killed her parents.

Evan raised his voice. "Everybody! Closer, get in closer. No matter what happens, we go through the gate!"

Sorel waved a hand at his men. They spread out to widen the interval between them. The courage of the crowd began to fail when they got within just a few frightening yards of the Taggert line. Men, women, and students turned left or right to separate themselves from the rapidly diminishing mass of moving targets.

"Nobody wants to get shot!" Dar whispered.

"Can't blame them," Evan replied. "Not looking forward to it myself."

Dar was mortified. "They wouldn't—"

"They would," he interrupted. "Probably just rock salt. If they shoot, just run!"

"Where?"

He pointed. "See? Go that way and you'll be in the forest within two or three miles. The other way takes you up the mountain."

"What's up there?" she asked, thinking about the locator in her pocket.

Evan slowed his pace. "Hell if I know! Taggerts are going to catch all kinds of crap for this. Come back in two days or so. They'll have to be gone or risk some jail time. It'll be okay."

"What about you?"

He smiled at her. "We'll still be here when you get back. Might have a few bruises, but trust me, you'll have something to talk about for a very time long time. Might even make you famous."

Dar stumbled when the crowd around her slowed. "My name is—"

"Don't tell me now!" Evan interrupted. "Wait until you get back, then tell me who you are. It'll be more fun that way!"

Sorel joined his hired guns to form a segmented line between the returning people and the gate in to their enclave. Men, women, and teens began to file through their ranks. Most of them looked away without speaking. Others were provocative; they taunted the Taggert men with rude gestures and verbal insults.

Evan began to lose his nerve when it became obvious to him that Dar would have to pass within arm's reach of Sorel or one of his men. "Back!" he warned her urgently. "Go back. Keep your head down and run!"

"There she is!" a male voice called out.

Dar turned to flee. She felt Evan's strong hands give her a push.

Sorel order his men to open fire.

Shotgun blasts pelted the dispersing crowd with a nonlethal combination of rock salt and rubber pellets. A dozen or more people screamed when they were hit by the blasts.

The sudden plunge into darkness was terrifying. Dar fumbled with the flashlight on her vest. It's bouncing beam wobbled and whirled as she ran. Racing away from the lighted gate, she fled through a maze of ramshackle buildings, hoping to get far from the enclave walls before anyone had a chance to see which way she'd gone.

* * *

Sorel planted his feet when he realized Evan was going to charge. He blocked a flurry of fists when the defensive teenager tried to punch him in the face. "You really don't want to do this!"

"Yes, I do!" Evan swore as he landed a solid blow.

Blood flowed from Sorel's nose. He sidestepped the next blow, grabbing Even's elbow and hand for leverage. He flipped the teen on his back with a swift, powerful lunge.

"Cease fire!" he bellowed. "Everybody stop shooting! She's gone, damn it! She's gone."

Evan hit the ground hard enough to knock the wind out of his lungs. He gasped for air as Sorel rallied his men.

"Which way did she go?"

"That way!" somebody yelled.

The one-eyed man looked around. It took several seconds for him to understand what his henchmen were trying to say.

The remaining enclave residents fled through the gate, into the comparative safety of their fortified town.

He didn't look at the men and women behind the barricades. He knew what they thought. "It's not going to go well for you if we find out she's in there!"

A large man in faded, woodland-patterned static camouflage looked right at him through a hole in the nearest sentry post. He spoke to somebody on a handheld radio.

Sorel knew that he and his hired guns would spend a cold night in outdoor lockup if they stayed much longer. As much of a risk taker as he was, he cautioned himself to remember that some finesse was needed to work around the locals. They reluctantly tolerated what he was doing only because the Taggert family could call on a large militia equipped with mortars, artillery, and enough armored vehicles to overwhelm their defenses.

He waved his arms to motivate his men. "Go, go, go!"

Evan scrambled to his feet as the last of the crowd went into the enclave. He kicked one of Sorel's men as he ran by.

The one-eyed man counted heads to be sure that all four of his cohorts were on their way. "I'm going to remember you!" he told Evan before bolting in to the darkness.

"Yeah, do that!" the angry teen spat. He looked at the guards behind their barricades. "Thanks for the help."

* * *

Dar slowed down, forcing herself to walk, rather than run, between dark structures, through open porticos, and across large, covered porches. Within just a few short minutes, gravel crunched under her boots. The beam of her flashlight made it easier to see that she was about to enter a cornfield. She looked askance at a quarter moon in the star-filled sky. "That's not going to tell a lot."

She turned off her flashlight and reached for the locator gadget in her vest pocket. Her mouth became suddenly parched when she saw the arrow swing casually to the west, in the direction of the tall corn. Shouting voices far behind her only added to the stress she felt in her tightening stomach. "Calm down," she told herself. "You've been chased before. This is no big deal."

Dar pressed the seek button on the gadget again, just to be sure. "Through the corn. Of course. No, wait. Stay on the road, follow the drainage ditches. Go around the corn! Not as fast, but much safer."

Pushing her dirty glasses back into place, Dar's eyes adjusted to the pale moonlight while she caught her breath. She took a breath and walked deliberately with the locator in her sweating hand. She passed over a drainage ditch on a swaying wooden footbridge. Arriving at an obvious intersection, she stopped to listen for pursuers.

She heard fewer voices. They seemed further away. In front of her, the high rise of Capitol Peak blotted out some of the stars.

Sounds of approaching automobile engines made her look back. She could make out the distinctive glow of headlights as a line of vehicles rolled down one of the access roads.

Dar followed the rough shoulder of the gravel road without turning on her flashlight. Anxiously relying on the locator, she turned at each intersection when it was necessary to change course.

"Don't run," she verbalized stoically. "No point in wearing yourself out."

The terrain got steeper as she made her way up a zigzagging trail to a terraced field. Travelling upward through three more terraces, she stopped to catch her breath next to a sign that was overgrown by bushes and weeds. "Capitol Peak National Forest," she read.

The idea seemed ludicrous. "Are you kidding me?" she panted while looking around. "They made all this a freakin' park? Why! Who plays out here? I am not having fun!"

Muscles in Dar's legs ached while she looked up resentfully at the elevation that still remained to be hiked. A glance over her shoulder allowed her to see the headlights of individual vehicles making their way up and down the cornfields. She counted four without being able to decide if they were cars or trucks.

"Doesn't really matter," she realized. "They'll figure out where I am soon enough."

Her apprehension grew when she saw a farmhouse in the distance, near what looked like a wide gravel road. Smoke from the chimney and lights in the windows made it clear that somebody was home. Moving as quietly as she could through tall grass, she sneaked around the place without losing sight of it. She deliberately walked at a steady pace over loose gravel on the road to avoid kicking any stones. There was enough moonlight for Dar to see signs of the winding uphill track through clumps of trees. It zigzagged up the mountain.

She looked down at the enclave. Its earthen walls and the surrounding community were visible from her vantage point in the foothills. The smell of cooking food wafted from the farmhouse as she lost sight of it. Scrounging through her rucksacks for more beef jerky, she ate while she walked along the side of the ascending road.

After an hour of hiking, she paused to rest her aching legs and look at the night sky. "More to see when you're higher up," she remembered from her studies.

According to her watch, Dar arrived at a plateau just after 3 a.m. She stared at a large, open area and the rustic ruins of a nearby flat-roofed structure for several seconds. A few yards beyond the tumbledown building, she could see the gravel road continue. It seemed to reach effortlessly up the forested mountain. A rusting metal guardrail skirted the open area, bracketed by four unpowered street lights.

Dar eyed the gravel under her feet with new interest. "No weeds," she observed through a long, strong yawn. "I remember reading that parks were a big deal. I didn't think anyone cared about them this much!"

She walked to the nearest portion of guard rail. Through a long, straight break in the trees that ran far down the mountain, she could make out the boundaries of tended fields and some of the access roads she'd walked on before hiking the mountain. Turning her attention to the remains of the manmade structure, she found a fallen sign leaned against the outer wooden wall near what might've been a doorway. She was able to read, "National Park Service. Visitor hours: 9 a.m. to 9 p.m. Permit required."

Dar unclipped her flashlight and turned it on. "You get one guess what I don't have."

Following the beam of her light, she probed the interior. Broken twigs and dead leaves covered old trash—cans, bottles, and food wrappers of all kinds. Wall supports and ceiling beams were blackened.

"Gutted by fire," she concluded.

As common as that debris was, something about the combination of factors made Dar take a closer look. Random holes in the roof let in some starlight, which only encouraged her curiosity. She kicked some of the refuse away with a swing of her foot. “Hm. This has to be the neatest mess I have ever seen.”

Filling her mouth with more jerky, she walked around the outside of the building. Weeds, bushes, and leaves were not piled up against any of the warped cedar planks that made up the structure’s outer walls. Near what she thought was the rear exit, Dar found footprints in soft earth.

“Well, okay. That settles it. Somebody has been coming here.”

Dar went back inside the ruin. Making her way down a short corridor, she emerged behind a long, wide counter. The remnants of a heat-shriveled plastic sign were hard to decipher through cobwebs.

“Customer service,” she guessed.

Her laugh was cut short when the beam of her light passed over a black electrical cord that was stapled to the nearest wall. Using her flashlight, she followed the cord out of the ground, up the charred, flaking wall, to where it connected to a small, black dome on the ceiling. “Great. More electronics,” she complained. “Hello! Anyone in there? Can you see me?”

Dar turned in place to look for more clues. The obvious lack of natural clutter and the presence of what could be powered electronics made sense when she remembered what she had seen in the abandoned Haven Site.

“You guys are hiding,” she concluded angrily.

The gadget in her vest beeped. She slapped the pocket it was in. “Not now! Be quiet. I’m trying to figure this out.”

The sound of an approaching automobile intruded on her thoughts. Bright headlights dazzled her when their beams blazed through dozens of holes all over the old building. They lit the interior for just a moment, allowing Dar to see there was no furniture inside.

Gravel crunched under rolling tires as the vehicle came to a stop. The headlights winked out as the engine was shut off. Squeaky doors opened. Casual conversation filled the air, just loud enough for her to guess there might be four men outside.

She turned off her flashlight and clipped it to her vest while trying to hear them talk. Closing her eyes to listen, she reached calmly for her shotgun. Kneeling out of sight behind the counter, she tried to understand what she was hearing.

CHAPTER SEVENTEEN

Sorel Taggert and three hired guns got out of the parked SUV. He leaned back inside to reach for a dangling radio microphone.

Frank's voice came from dashboard speakers. "You want me to drive the lake shore again?"

Sorel keyed the mic. "Do it. Look into every possibility. That's why I'm up here."

"How's the view?"

Taggert made a series of gestures with one hand that told the armed men with him to spread out and begin their search.

"We drove up an old access road. Not sure how far up we are. There is an old building close by." He paused to squint through the darkness. "Looks like the road goes up further."

Frank chuckled through the connection. "You think she up there?"

The experienced tracker watched his men fan out and disappear into the foliage. "Most fugitives are smart enough to avoid high places. They know they have to come back down, eventually. Being on the top of a mountain is like being cornered. They almost always have enough survival instinct to avoid that mistake."

Frank spoke to somebody off mic. "I gotta go. The locals are turning out their police and volunteer militia."

Sorel looked at his wristwatch. "Fine. Just be sure everyone does finish their sweep. No slacking! I'll beat the bushes up here for a while. When you see

Partridge, tell him to expect me for breakfast. With any luck, our problem is long gone."

"You know what Seth is going to say about that!"

The pragmatic man shrugged. "Be positive. She's been scared away from the school. Sooner or later, she's going to turn up and somebody will tell us what we need to know. They always do."

"Roger. Out."

Sorel put the warm radio microphone on the cluttered dashboard. He was reaching for a flashlight when gunfire erupted from somewhere behind the moldy, ruined building. He reached into the back seat for an automatic rifle as a second volley of shots echoed through the trees. Standing upright, he moved a few steps away from the SUV while releasing the safety on his weapon. "Norris, Martel—somebody talk to me!"

He turned in place, slowly sweeping the long barrel of his rifle in search of targets. Thoughts of ambush crossed his mind. As unlikely as it seemed, the girl might have come up to this elevation in search of a good choke point, where she could hide and fire on anyone who came looking for her. A third series of shots made it abundantly clear to him that somebody had found all three of his henchmen.

* * *

Dar raised her head when the shooting stopped. She crouched to peer over the edge of the counter. She began to hear soft footfalls outside the rear of the ruined building. They approached the back door—and stopped.

Feeling her body tense with fear, Dar slipped away from the counter and back down the short hallway. Night air blew in through the open door. She forced herself to take measured breaths while raising her shotgun. With one hand on the trigger and the other on the pump action, she waited.

* * *

Sorel ran to the nearest corner of the old building and flung himself against the wall. There was just enough predawn twilight for him to see a humanoid shape sprawled on the ground nearby. He recognized one of his men from the color of their boots and pants. He was on his back, wearing a dazed look on his face.

Sorel's detail-oriented mind quickly noticed that the hired gun had three small cylindrical objects sticking out of his left arm. "Darts," he realized.

He held his rifle ready and raised his voice. "Hey! Whoever you are, I don't want any trouble! We are— um— out here looking for a dangerous criminal. We didn't know this was your turf. Can you hear me?"

His ears heard the rhythmic noise of area insects and movement inside the building. Sorel pointed his rifle and moved stealthily along the side of the structure, toward what he hoped would be a rear entrance.

Turning the corner, he almost tripped over the body of another hired gun. He was face down in the grass, still holding his pistol with one hand. Sorel nudged him with the toe of his boot. The unconscious man moaned.

"Well," he mumbled to himself, "that answers my next question. Whoever you are, you've got a thing about killing. Don't want to do it unless you have to. Good to know."

Sorel quietly stepped over the comatose man. Looking left and right, he scrutinized his surroundings for anything that might be out of place. "Okay, you made your point!" he shouted. "Come on. Let's be reasonable about this! Say something!"

* * *

Dar became angry when she heard Sorel's voice. Seeing his slow-moving shadow pass by several holes in the nearby wall increased her outrage as she watched him getting closer. Growing rage caused her to overlook his behavior. She didn't care who he was talking to, only that he was coming closer to the open doorway where she lurked.

As livid as she was, some part of her thought about the deadly shotgun in her hands and Bellamy's police badge in her pocket. Conflicting emotions somehow unlocked a painful memory.

The last time she'd seen her parents alive, they were defiantly standing back-to-back in the dark living room of the happy home they'd worked so hard to make, with shotguns in their hands.

Deep down inside her aching heart, Dar knew she had to do more than take revenge. She laid her weapon down on the dirty floor and reached for the folding metal shovel that was lashed to her rucksack.

"Come a little closer, I've got something for you…"

* * *

Nearby bushes rustled. Sorel made a note of the sound and the direction it came from without looking at the source. Increasing twilight allowed him to perceive the rear door he'd been looking for. He remained motionless while his mind worked out the details. He appeared to be at a disadvantage against one, or even two, defenders who were in hiding.

"Come on! I know you can hear me!"

Somewhere in the nearby gloom, a masculine voice responded. "I can see you, too. Put the rifle down and step away from it. Do it, now!"

Sorel laid the automatic rifle on the ground and stepped over it. He raised both hands while taking one more step toward the rear entrance, where he could see part of the open door and a hallway beyond. He turned toward his unseen opponent.

"Okay, you got me."

He was about to say something diplomatic when he was unexpectedly surprised by a loud angry scream from behind! He spun around, just in time to see Dar emerge from the building with a folding shovel gripped in both hands.

"Murderer!" she shrieked, bludgeoning him with the implement.

Sorel staggered backward with his arms raised to protect his ears and face. He gave ground with each heavy blow she inflicted. The blunt-force trauma of each strike rapidly wore him out. His arms fell limp as she swung with all her strength to hit him in the face. He fell to the ground with a loud thump.

Dar was still trying to catch her breath when a big flashlight beam shined in her face.

"Calm down," a male voice told her through the glare. "I don't know what your problem was with him, but it's over now."

She threw away the shovel. "He killed my family!"

"I believe you," the obscured man affirmed. "Now, please, just calm down or we will have to make you sleep for a while. You are—"

Dar turned when she heard movement. "Stay back! I'll shoot anyone who comes near me. Who are you people?"

He tried to be reassuring. "You made it. This is the place you were looking for."

She put a hand on her pistol. "I'm really not in the mood for jokes."

"Okay," he laughed. "You've got something in your pocket that helped you get here. Please, take it out and have a look."

Dar opened a vest pocket. She used one hand to grab and hold the locator gadget while trying to shield her eyes from the flashlight beam with the other. The digital arrow was gone. In its place was one word: Arrived.

"I really do hate this thing," she griped.

The man she couldn't see through the glare laughed. "We're glad to see you, too."

He lowered his beam to the ground. Illumination scattered to form a halo of diffuse light around him—and three more men dressed just like him.

Dar couldn't help noticing they wore crisp, clean, static woodland camouflage and matching face paint. Patches and insignia on their uniforms didn't mean anything to her. They carried guns she didn't recognize. All of them were equipped with a camo-patterned rucksack, much like her own.

"This is a Haven Site?"

The talkative man came closer. He stepped effortlessly over Sorel's splayed limp form.

"Yes, I suppose it would be easier to think of it that way."

The light in his hand allowed her to get a better look at him. He appeared to be in his late thirties or early forties.

One of the people with him used a handheld radio. "Sentry One-Bravo; approach is secure. Tell the medic we have four to be processed."

A female voice replied through the handset. "How is the new arrival?"

The radio operator looked at Sorel. "She's fine, which is more than I can say for the Tango who was dumb enough to follow her. Tell the medic to bring lots of ice."

Dar looked askance at the authoritative man standing in front of her.

His bearing and attitude was reassuring. "Don't worry about it. You're safe now."

"What about—"

"Please," he interrupted. "We'll put some food in you and let you rest. Then, you'll get as many answers as we can give you."

Dar watched two of the camouflaged men move Sorel into a sitting position, with his back to the wall of the building.

"What about him and his men?"

The assertive man gave his light to one of the nearby soldiers. "They're going to live, if that's what you're asking. Our medic will make sure they have no untreated injuries. Then, she'll give each of them a shot. It's a fast-acting drug causing a form of amnesia. They're going to 'lose' the last 24 hours. When they wake up, they'll have a good reason to believe they've been in a car crash."

"Okay."

He looked her in the eye. "Is that all right with you?"

Dar watched Sorel begin to regain consciousness. He was groggy.

"I didn't really want to kill him," she admitted. "I was just hoping for—you know— I wanted him to answer for what he did. My mother, my father, and my brother. I owe them that much."

He looked at Sorel, then at Dar. "I know you do. I also think they'd be proud of what you've done to get this far. It's a little hard to explain right now, but trust me. Guys like him have a way of getting what they deserve."

"I wanted to be the one—"

He put a warm encouraging hand on her shoulder. "Who knows? You might be. The future is a funny thing. You really might be the one who does make him answer for what he's done. For now, let's get breakfast. A lot of people are waiting to meet you."

Dar watched as two of the uniformed men bound Sorel's arms and legs with clear plastic zip ties. Exhaustion and euphoria overpowered some of her outrage and grief, enough to let her think more clearly.

"My parents liked to say that we make the future we want to live in. I'm starting to understand what that means and why they said it. Yeah, let's go eat. I have a big appetite and a lot of questions."

* * *

Sorel became lucid several minutes later. He looked up to see a woman wearing static woodland camouflage and face paint. He struggled against his bonds when she held up a syringe. "Hey, wait a minute! I can explain—"

She stuck the needle into his arm through his shirt sleeve and pushed the plunger. "Don't fight it."

He was able to make out half a dozen people around him, all wearing the same camo and face paint. Some of them carried battery-powered lights that illuminated the area around them enough for him to see all three of the hired guns who'd come with him. They were laid out on the ground, in a row, faces turned up with their arms at their sides.

More details became apparent when he looked for them. All six of the people around him carried automatic weapons. Military shoulder patches and insignias were briefly visible to him in the swaying lamp light whenever they turned away from him.

The drugs he'd been injected with burned in his veins; the irritation spread throughout his body. Strength and vigor began to drain from his body while he remembered the old, yellow piece of paper he'd found during his pursuit of Dar. He hadn't considered the possibility that she was the person who must have dropped it. Unfolding it, reading the words, and later being laughed at by his brother Ben; all of it came back in a surge of understanding that made him lightheaded.

He looked unsteadily at the kneeling camouflaged woman who had just injected him. "The insignia on your collar; you're an officer."

She reached out a hand to keep him from falling over. "It doesn't matter. Whatever you think you see, all of it will be gone when you wake up."

He grasped feebly with his bound hands to touch her wrist. "Army."

She laid his limp hands in his lap and stood up.

"Don't go." He gasped with the effort to stay awake. "We're on your side. My brother is the elected mayor of Tumwater. We're enforcing the last emergency disaster declaration."

Sorel's vision began to distort. A fuzzy figure came closer, holding Dar's folding shovel in their hands.

"Ah. That man has a hard head. See? Right here, the blade of this shovel has a notch in it!"

Sorel Taggert passed out hearing laughter. He slumped to the grass with a smudge of camouflage paint smeared on his right hand.

* * *

Shortly after sunrise, a search party led by Frank found Sorel and his hired guns in the twisted wreck of their SUV, at the bottom of a ravine near the foothills of Capitol Peak. The local physician who examined all four passengers said their survival was miraculous. "They'd all be dead if they hadn't been wearing their seat belts."

Sorel was lethargic when rescuers lifted him onto a waiting stretcher.

"The last thing I remember is waiting for the girl at Partridge's house. We sent out trackers with dogs. Has anyone heard back from them?"

Frank sat nearby while medics dressed Sorel's many cuts and bruises. "Looks like you planted you face in the steering wheel."

Sorel was confused. He put trembling fingers to his swollen face.

"What's that?" Frank pointed at the dark smear on Sorel's hand.

The one-eyed man raised his hand for a closer look. "It's camo paint. The same stuff we use for special operations. Where did this come from?"

"It's on your hand. You tell me."

Sorel was intrigued by the dark green smudge. He reached into one of his pockets for a handkerchief. He looked at Frank while thoroughly wiping his hand. "Does it seem strange to you that we crashed like this?"

Frank waited for a busy medic to move out of the way, he tried to hide his laugh. "Did you have the headlights on?"

Sorel grimaced. "I can't remember."

Frank craned his neck to see what was left of the overturned SUV. "You know what? Doesn't matter. I'm just glad you're alive. You could have broken your neck, or worse. All of you could be dead. Let the medics work. You'll be out of here soon enough."

Sorel was uncharacteristically speechless for several seconds. He kept glancing at the stain on his handkerchief. "All of us survived this crash? How is that possible?"

Frank stood up. "Get some rest. I'll ride with you all the way back to Tumwater."

Nobody was surprised when the astonished doctor declared that all the crash victims had suffered from severe concussions that robbed them of their short-term memories.

"Only time will tell how much of it is permanent brain injury. They'll be lucky men if all they lose track of is a single day."

CHAPTER EIGHTEEN

Dar spent the night under clean sheets in a Quonset hut near the top of Capitol Peak. Shortly after 7:30 a.m., she was given freshly laundered clothing and escorted to breakfast by a physician's assistant.

Gaffney was a tall woman with a mild disposition and a lot of questions for Dar, most of which related to her diet and medical history.

After a brief walking tour, they ate by themselves in a large designated mess hall. "Everybody comes here to eat," Gaffney explained while Dar destroyed a plate of toast. "You're allowed to have three meals a day, whenever you want."

Dar pushed her glasses back in to place before devouring more bacon. "This place isn't what I expected. Not even close. Just a few buildings, just a few people. Some kids, not many. Why do you have so many radio antennas and satellite dishes?"

"You know what those are?"

Dar nodded through a drink of juice. "Yeah. You might not know this, but there's a whole lot of stories about places like this floating around out there."

Gaffney made notations on a touchscreen computer tablet. "What do you think about those stories, now that you're here?"

Dar put her fork down, she frowned. "It's real."

"What's wrong?" Gaffney asked.

The young woman struggled physically with her thoughts. "How can you sit there with a tablet in your hand like it's no big deal? I was always taught—"

The PA put the device aside. "That computer is completely safe to use. We have a lot of explaining to do. There's a lot you deserve to know. Is anything about this place familiar to you? Anything at all?"

Dar shrugged as a dozen people walked by her table on their way to the serving line. "You asked me the same question earlier. This is not the kind of place I could forget. Who would want to?"

Gaffney looked at her tablet, then at Dar. "What you like to call the 'myth' of Haven is something we take seriously. When the world fell apart, the memory of what all of this is and what it was for…faded. As hard as it might be to believe, a lot of what your grands told you was the truth. AI revolts, terrorism; even the part about rampaging robot hordes. Time passed and the people who worked in places like this inevitably lost contact with their governments. From then on, they've just been trying to do the right thing."

Dar looked over her shoulder at the men and women around her. "I did think it had something to do with helping. Why do so many people keep on saying this is one place, when it's really a lot of them, scattered all over?"

Gaffney ate some fruit off her own breakfast plate. "The hard truth is, we don't know. There's a lot of guesses that sound good. They all have something do to with our need for attainability. People feel like it's easier to achieve their goals when they believe there is only one thing to find or to do. It's not logical, but it is empathic. Say what you want about our species—after all, our ancestors did wreck the world—but we are here now, and we've got a chance to choose differently."

"How?"

Gaffney winked. "Start by keeping the secret. People who are positively motivated will eventually go on to do good things. No matter what they believe in, if it really is for the greater good, they'll work hard to make it happen."

"Is that what you do here? Keep the secret so the rest of us have something to believe?"

The doctor-in-training smiled. "Yes, with a twist. This place really was a Haven Site. Its job was to maintain satellite, cell phone, and internet for most of Washington. Refugee transition camps, like the one you found, were set up to help people get out of the big cities. They ran out of supplies or they got looted. Eventually, a decision was made to turn off the cell towers and satellite dishes."

"Robots?"

Gaffney nodded. "Any hostile technology that could find us might report our location to something—anything—that could come here and kill us. So, we've just been keeping most of it ready…like for a rainy day."

Dar pointed up. "For as long as I can remember, it's rained a lot in this part of the world. You need a better example."

"Fair enough," Gaffney snickered. "So. Are you ready to go have the big talk with our big boss?"

"No," Dar confessed while eating. "I don't understand. Why do I have to leave?" she mumbled with her mouth full. "Everyone I meet says I can stay. Why can't I go to school here?"

Gaffney spread her hands. "For what it is, this compound is really quite crowded. Just small enough to be hidden by all those trees; not large enough to be seen by the people in Delphi."

Dar was astonished. "They don't know you're here?"

Gaffney shrugged. "Do you know what an open secret is?"

"Something everybody knows, but they just don't talk about it."

"It's like that," Gaffney affirmed. "Anyone who does know what's on this mountain chooses to keep it to themselves. For any number of reasons, the people who do suspect what's going on up here won't say anything. Even if you did want to tell the truth about what you've seen, who would believe you?"

Dar thought about Marsh and his room full of dubious clues.

The observant woman pushed her serving tray aside. "Relax. I don't think you're going to give us away. You have a lot of your parents in you. Some of your grandfather, too. Haven't you wondered why your father had a locator in with the rest of his things?"

Dar turned in her seat so she could see more of the mess hall. "They were here?"

"Your grandparents were," Gaffney explained. "After the resettlement camp closed, your grandfather came here with his wife. We have a few pictures on file. Are you sure he never said anything about this place?"

Dar was overcome with admiration. "Not one word." She looked at her benefactor. "They were good people. You know what I mean? Both of them passed when I was little. Jack used to love their stories, especially when my grandpa talked about the machines. I never did understand how anything made by human hands could be that ferocious and terrible. Where does my father fit in to this?"

Gaffney drank the last of her juice. "He grew up knowing our secret and he kept it. At some point, he must have told your mother. I can't imagine he would keep a thing like that from her. They were probably waiting for just the right moment to tell you."

Dar looked down at the crumbs and smeared egg yolk on her mostly empty plate. "No, there has to be more. What's the point in keeping that kind of secret? What did they ever do with it?"

Gaffney could sense Dar's growing anxiety. "Did you ever see your grandparents help anyone?"

"Sure, all the time."

"What about your parents," Gaffney asked. "What did you see them do for the people around them?"

Dar hesitated. "They…gave food to our neighbors when their crops didn't come in. We gave away some of our piglets when people around us lost their hogs to parasites. Sometimes, my mother would invite somebody's young son or daughter to stay with us while their parents took care of some difficult business."

Gaffney was emphatic. "That's a lot of work. Why do you think they did so much?"

Dar snorted. "We helped them and they helped us, that's how it works."

"What about the Taggerts?"

Dar's jaw clenched. "Yeah, okay. You've got me there. It wasn't always like that. I didn't hear the name Taggert until I was ten or twelve years old. I only just recently found out that my mother was related to them. We did well enough. Everybody was getting by. Taggerts came to visit our farm two or three times a year, then once a month. They wanted us to pay taxes. That's what my dad told me. There was no way for me or Jack to know. We never imagined it would end like this."

Gaffney softened her tone. "It's okay. None of it was your fault. With a little help, you can do something to make this right."

"Like what?"

The serious woman leaned over. She lowered her voice. "Go get yourself educated, then look for anyone who has, in some way, been harmed by the Taggerts of this world and be the one who helps them. Do just that much and you will always have a home on this mountain."

"Sounds like you have friends all over the place."

Gaffney was in no mood to be coy. "We don't have a national government to back us anymore. It's just us. When we can, we go out there and we try our best to do something for the greater good! Some of us farm; others wear a badge. A few of us have even built railroads through the forest. Who knows what you'll contribute? Only time can tell."

Dar thought about the clattering train and Officer Bellamy. "So, there's a bunch of us all over the place. Is that right?"

Gaffney laughed. "Nobody knows for sure. Technicians who keep the radios going say our antennas sometimes pick up low-powered signals from far away Haven Sites. Nothing conclusive; just enough traffic to suggest they are out there. In the meantime, we work with the friends we have."

"Does that include Delphi and Belmore?"

Gaffney stood up. "No comment. Come on, let's go. The boss can fill you in on all that hero stuff. Trust me, in a few days you'll be so bored with this place, you'll want to be out of here and on your way to school."

* * *

Dar's fascination with the high-altitude sanctuary diminished over the next two days.

"I feel out of place," Dar told Gaffney at dinner during the second night. "I know I can fit in eventually. I just need to grow up a little. You know what I mean. Learn something and find a job."

"You don't like our farm?" Gaffney joked.

Dar's expression changed. "This is a lot harder to explain," she muddled while eating strawberries. "I never said anything to anyone, not even my parents, but— I've always thought my future was out there somewhere. That's maybe a bad choice of words, but I still think I should go out there, into the world."

"After you finish school?" Gaffney prodded.

"Yes!" Dar emphasized with a nod. "My parents wore many hats. They grew food and made stuff. Jack was always going to be the farmer, not me. That's just who I am."

The older woman relaxed. "I'm only about ten years older than you are, so let me give you some advice. Everything we live through leaves a mark on us. We can be changed for better or worse; it's all in what we do with that experience. Your family has just been murdered. You can go do some killing of your own, maybe settle a few scores. Or, you can learn what you need to know and go 'out there' somewhere to make a better mark on somebody who hasn't suffered the same kind of losses."

Dar was embarrassed. "I've thought about it. Believe me, I have! I am no killer. It's not what my parents or my grandparents would want for me. As much as he liked stories with blood and guts, Jack wouldn't want me to be the same thing that hurt us."

She recovered her composure. "I've already done terrible things for the sake of survival. They will take some time to live with. I remember my grandfather saying something like that about the things he had to face. I will go to school, then—maybe—I will look in to being a police officer."

"Not many of them around these days," Gaffney observed solemnly.

Dar agreed with the sentiment. "I know. Which reminds me, I have some things that need to be taken back to Belmore."

Gaffney ate slowly while she chatted. "Well, that shouldn't be much of a problem. You've still got at least four weeks before the next academic term starts. The train gets you there and back, with time to spare."

* * *

Ten days later, Dar got off the train in Belmore dressed in her own clean clothes. She wore her multi-pocket vest, carrying only her father's rucksack and few belongings. A discreet inquiry at the nearest guarded gate to the enclave caused Officers Hicks and Monroe to turn up while she was eating a hot dog.

"What is it with you and food?" Hicks heckled.

Monroe was more dramatic. "Haven't you already done enough damage?"

Dar laughed, eating while she talked. "It's good to see you guys!"

Hicks made a show of looking around. "Good to see you, too. You had us worried. We did get a report from Delphi. We know about Bellamy."

She threw away the greasy wrapper when she was finished. "That's why I'm here. I have her badge, her gun, and a report. She wrote it by hand, before— you know. I really am so sorry about all of this!"

The officers took turns hugging her. "Drake will be glad to get her shield back," Monroe reassured her. "Just so you know, old One-Eye came through here a while back. He was busted up pretty bad. Hicks and I have a bet going with the others. We think it was you who laid him out. We'll cut you in for a share; all you need to do is tell us—"

Dar's faux humility was unconvincing. "He had it coming. I beat him like a drum."

"Thought so," Hicks crowed. "We are going to be rich!"

Dar put a hand on his shoulder. "I don't want it. Please, give it to Bellamy's family. They're going to need money more than I do."

"What about school?" Monroe inquired while watching the crowd pass around them.

She smiled. "My parents took care of all that. They were always looking out for me. In some ways, they still are."

Hicks pointed at the guarded gate. "You've got one and a half Taggerts to your credit. That makes you a celebrity in this town! Come on inside with us. I'm sure the captain would like to hear all this straight from the source."

Dar unholstered her semiautomatic pistol and gave it to him. "I would like that!"

Monroe walked beside her. "I remember liking high school. Never was any good at the homework, but I liked it."

"He's not any good with paperwork now!" Hicks chimed in while following Dar. "Four years goes pretty fast, what are you going to do after graduation?"

High overcast parted; warm sun began to shine. She put her arms around both men. "I was thinking about a career in law enforcement."

CHAPTER NINETEEN

Cool wind blew across Black Lake in mid-September, shaking trees and foliage in and around the enclave of Delphi. Under the light of a single bulb, Dar unpacked her things in the small, second-story room of a girls' dormitory. Through an open window, she could see the 200-year-old school house that was the center of the campus. From what she'd been told, that historical site was the inspiration for the post-Collapse education facility she now attended.

The new, locally-made clothes she had on felt just as brand new as they were itchy. Moving around the room relieved some of the irritation, though not enough to satisfy her. She did try to feel better by silently reminding herself that the pants and shirt were not any kind of official school uniform. As many rules as the school at Delphi did enforce, the teachers and faculty did not make everyone dress the same way.

Opening a pocket on her vest, she tenderly removed her old, improvised eyeglasses. So much had happened in the last nine weeks, she'd almost forgotten about them. Standing next to a small wooden desk, she cleaned the scarred lenses with a soft cloth. She laid them between the study lamp and an electric alarm clock, where she could always see them. Hanging the last of her clothes in a narrow closet, she paused to gaze at her reflection in a wall-mounted mirror.

The eyes that looked back at her through steel-rimmed glasses were still haunted. Faint bags under her eyes proved still she wasn't sleeping very well, despite the safety of her new surroundings. Behind her, she saw a small wooden bookshelf that was filled with the semester's planned reading. She couldn't decide if the sight of those worn textbooks was a good thing or an unwanted reminder of what she missed.

A knock on the open door shocked her out of the past.

Evan leaned in. "Helen is looking for you."

Dar looked at the alarm clock on her desk. She fled from the room with a stream of curses.

Evan silently watched her go. He shut the door to her room and went downstairs.

With rules and first impressions still on her troubled mind, Dar ran out of the building as fast as she could go. Her new shoes clopped across the open ground, making it hard for her to leap over a low hedge when it got in her way. Dodging between people who were quite surprised to see her come and go, she bolted in to Helen's office as a clock on the wall showed 8:30 a.m.

"I'm not late!"

Helen looked up from her desk, pausing to push some of her gray curls back into place. "I hope not. That's why I sent someone to remind you."

"Class doesn't start until 9," Dar explained while catching her breath.

The teacher put down her pen. She tugged on the sleeves of her dress. Dar noticed the gesture; she smoothed some of the wrinkles out of her own clothes.

"What have I done wrong now?"

Helen smiled before she stood up. "Far from it. I just came from the administrator's office. They tell me you paid your tuition in full and up front. That's very commendable. They also told me you overpaid."

She came closer to hand Dar a stack of gold coins. "I'm sure these were for Jack," she said compassionately while softly pressing six double-eagles into the stunned student's hand. "I'm so sorry for doing this. It must be an unwanted reminder of what you've been through. Your parents worked hard. Think of these coins as their legacy."

"I already have," Dar confessed quietly.

Helen went back to her desk. "Please, see to it soon. A sum of money that large could get anyone in trouble, even you. From here on out, you are the only person who can hold yourself back or ruin your plans."

"I know."

Helen sat. "I know you do, but I still have to say it. That scuffle you had at the gate with the Taggert men; it has certainly made you famous with the students. Evan thinks quite highly of you. He never misses a chance to show off his scars from the rock salt. I'll have to say something to him about that."

"My point is," she emphasized, "You have given the faculty several good reasons to notice what you do. I know you can take good care of yourself, but please, no heroics inside the walls of this enclave. Certainly not on school grounds!"

Dar giggled. "Do they know how you faced down Sorel Taggert and his men with your six-guns?"

Helen was indignant. "No, they don't. It should stay that way."

"Would you get fired?"

The experienced educator sighed. She folded her hands on the desk in front of her. "Dar, this is a school. You're here to learn and I'm here to teach. Can you imagine how distracting it would be for everyone if they knew what you did when you're not here?"

Dar looked around Helen's small, sparse office. The image it projected of the teacher was nothing like she was familiar with. Diplomas and photos hung on the walls; shelves were full of battered books. There was no sign of the distinctive, bold, blue leather coat and matching wide brimmed hat that Helen customarily wore when she was "teaching."

She stammered, “Yeah, right. Guns have to stay in the armory when we’re here. Why don’t you want anyone to know—?”

Helen laid her hands flat. “I don’t want them to be afraid of me or to have unrealistic expectations about what I can do. Dar, I’m not as young as I look. I won’t always be fast enough to stop the bad actors like Sorel Taggert. Everyone who comes here to learn must have the chance to do so without feeling pressured to do things that stand a good chance of getting them hurt.”

“Or killed,” Dar added soberly.

A push-button telephone on Helen’s desk rang. She answered it while Dar absorbed the importance of the moment. Empathically, she knew her long-time teacher and mentor was right.

Helen hung up the corded receiver. “I’ve just been told that an old friend of yours has turned up in the school gardens. If you’re quick about it, you can see them before class begins. Please, hurry!”

Dar excused herself and went to that part of the school where experienced farmers and ranchers taught outdoors on tilled land or inside warm, moist greenhouses. Wending her way through racks of tools and shelves filled with seedlings, she looked for every clock in her path that she could see.

Teachers and assistants pointed her in the right direction when they saw her coming. “Over by the cabbage,” one of them told her.

Dar’s curiosity diminished. She suspected somebody was playing a prank on her.

“Over there,” a student holding a rake pointed, “Can’t miss ‘em.”

Dar stopped to take a breath. The structured schedule she was learning to live with was more binding than she thought it would be. She promised herself to take the joke in stride, no matter what it was. Passing through a covered workspace, she emerged to see Gerry the cow indulgently munching a head of cabbage.

As thrilled as she was to see the errant bovine, Dar was also mortified to realize that Gerry had more than a dozen cheerful witnesses to her crime. Men, women, and students stood nearby with smiles on their faces. Their applause made Dar blush.

After everything she'd been through, Gerry was not impressed or put off by the show. She stood at the end of a cultivated row, without leaving any footprints in the rich soil. Her hairy hide was matted with mud, sticks, and leaves. Despite an earlier protest, somebody she didn't know had washed some of the reeking mess off her flank, revealing the distinctive Lambert family brand. A few mouthfuls of her favorite food was the least she was entitled to.

Dar rushed ebulliently to hug the exhausted cow without caring about the wet grime that clung to her clothes. "I'm so glad to see you! Where have you been?"

Gerry exhaled with exasperation through her nostrils. She leaned close to Dar, almost knocking her down.

"I know!" Dar soothed while clinging to the muddy gratified cow, "How in the world did you find me?"

An older man wearing dirty overalls stepped out of the crowd. He took off his gloves. "I can answer that. We take the cows outside the enclave walls just about every day before sunrise to graze them where we can. She merged in with the herd when we brought them back early this morning. It's funny, when you think about it. We didn't know we had an extra until we started milking."

Dar staggered away from Gerry to get her footing. She steadied herself with one hand on the broad shoulder of the relaxing animal.

"Thanks, everyone! Gerry means a lot to me. I never thought I'd see her again."

The livestock handler came closer. "Don't get too excited. You'll have to get some kind of permission from somebody to keep her here. I'm just a wrangler. I don't know what the rule is on pets or— um— unusual family members, but I'm sure we can work out something."

Gerry finished off the head of cabbage she'd been eating while Dar picked leaves and twigs off her shirt. "Yeah, right. Rules. I am…not going to make it to class on time, am I? Could somebody please—"

Helen moved through the crowd. Careful about where she stepped, she approached Dar. "I had to see it for myself. I just had to see it. Well, Miss Lambert, what have you got to say for yourself?"

Dar caught sight of Capitol Peak in the distance. She scratched Gerry's ear. "I'm glad she's okay. Last time I saw her, you—I mean, we—were busy. We had stuff to do. Now that she is here, I'd like to make room for her. She needs a home as much as I do."

Helen surveyed the mood of the crowd behind her. "In all the years I've been here, this has never come up. Students have been known to bring cats or dogs. We've always accommodated them—within limits, of course. I'd be willing to advocate for you, but you'd have to attend your studies and take care of her at the same time. She does provide milk; that will be welcome. I hope you will be just as responsible."

Dar was relieved. "No problem. I've been cleaning up after her for years. Can she help with my homework?"

INDEX

Lightning Source UK Ltd.
Milton Keynes UK
UKHW022118200921
390927UK00002B/357

9 781935 964650